"I have something to tell you," Nina said.

"What?"

"I'm going away to college in the fall."

I felt both bad and good, all mixed together. I had put off telling her about New College because things were so bleak for her at home. I'd thought she had no chance to go to college.

"Where?" I said.

"To Antioch—you know, in Ohio. Dad has a friend on the faculty, an old classmate. He talked to him about me, and found out that, with my grades, I could get a scholarship, and a job to help support me."

"That's great, Nina! I'm so glad for you."

"But what about you?" she said. I told her, and it turned out that she had withheld the news from me for the same reason. I think we knew, somehow, that we were not ready to tie our lives together any more closely. We put out the fire, slung our skates over our shoulders, and started back to her house.

"I wonder," she said, "what we'll remember of this time, if we ever grow old."

ALSO BY MILTON MELTZER

The Landscape of Memory

The Rescuers:
The Story of the Gentiles Who Saved Jews in the Holocaust

Never to Forget: The Jews of the Holocaust

The American Revolutionaries:
A History in Their Own Words, 1750–1800

Voices from the Civil War

Mary McLeod Bethune: Voice of Black Hope

Winnie Mandela: The Soul of South Africa

Betty Friedan: A Voice for Women's Rights

Dorothea Lange: Life Through the Camera

George Washington and the Birth of Our Nation

Mark Twain: A Writer's Life

Poverty in America

Crime in America

Ain't Gonna Study War No More:
The Story of America's Peace Seekers

The Black Americans:
A History in Their Own Words

The Jewish Americans:
A History in Their Own Words

Columbus and the World Around Him

The Bill of Rights:
How We Got It and What It Means

The American Promise:
Voices from a Changing Nation

Benjamin Franklin: The New American

1922

1918

1932

1932

Starting from Home
A Writer's Beginnings

A MEMOIR BY
MILTON MELTZER

Puffin Books

The chapter opening pages were designed by Virginia Norey.

PUFFIN BOOKS
Published by the Penguin Group
Viking Penguin, a division of Penguin Books USA Inc.,
375 Hudson Street, New York, New York 10014, U.S.A.
Penguin Books Ltd, 27 Wrights Lane, London W8 5TZ, England
Penguin Books Australia Ltd, Ringwood, Victoria, Australia
Penguin Books Canada Ltd, 2801 John Street, Markham, Ontario, Canada L3R 1B4
Penguin Books (N.Z.) Ltd, 182–190 Wairau Road, Auckland 10, New Zealand

Penguin Books Ltd, Registered Offices: Harmondsworth, Middlesex, England

First published in the United States of America by Viking Penguin Inc., 1988
Published in Puffin Books, 1991
1 3 5 7 9 10 8 6 4 2
Copyright © Milton Meltzer, 1988
All rights reserved

CRACKER JACK® Caramel-Coated Popcorn and Peanuts is a trademark of Borden,
Inc. Historical package on page 41 printed with permission of Borden, Inc. Photo of
Babe Ruth on page 53, courtesy of UPI/Bettmann News Photos; cartoon on page
65, courtesy of *The Toledo Blade*; photo on page 107, courtesy of Underwood and
Underwood/The Bettmann Archives; photo on page 117, courtesy of UPI/Bettmann
News Photos; poster on page 133, courtesy of the Museum of The City of
New York

LIBRARY OF CONGRESS CATALOGING IN PUBLICATION DATA
Meltzer, Milton, 1915–   Starting from home: a writer's beginnings /
by Milton Meltzer.   p. cm.
Originally published: New York, N.Y., U.S.A., : Viking Kestrel, 1988.
Summary: The author recounts the discoveries, hardships, and triumphs
of his early life and the influences that shaped him as a person and writer.
ISBN 0-14-032299-X
1. Meltzer, Milton, 1915–   —Juvenile literature.   2. Historians—
United States—Biography—Juvenile literature.   3. Writing—
Juvenile literature.   [1. Meltzer, Milton, 1915–   . 2. Authors,
American.]   I. Title.
[E175.5.M45A3   1991]
973'.07202—dc20   [B]   [92]   90-42261

Printed in the United States of America
Set in Sabon

To the memory of Anna Shaughnessy

ACKNOWLEDGMENTS

Grateful acknowledgment is made to the Picture Collection of the New York Public Library for illustrations on pages 41, 53, 65, 75, 107, 117, 133.

I owe special thanks to many people in Worcester for their generous assistance of several kinds: to Rose Barker, Frances Shaughnessy, Dorothy M. Gleason, Norma Feingold, Philip J. Philbin, David Porter, Beverly Osborn, Joyce Ann Tracy, James Mooney, Paul Brosnihan, Nancy Gaudette, Albert B. Southwick, Dolores Courtemanche, and Michael Silver.

To my brothers, Allan and Marshall, and my aunt Lee Berger, my loving thanks for sharing memories and adding family photos.

And to my editor, Deborah Brodie, heartfelt thanks for planting the seed and nursing its growth.

CONTENTS

Roots—
or Twigs

Me

My
Grandparents

Culver Pictures

Who was I? No, I don't mean the man who's writing these words down, but the child who was born soon after the twentieth century began. Was he me? The me I am today? Or someone so different in an early photo that I hardly recognize him: small, skinny, wavy brown hair, green eyes, straight nose, pale skin, thin arms and chest encased in a khaki shirt, and an uneasy smile as he looks into my eyes.

That's the boy on the outside. Inside was a being no one knew but himself. And often he was not sure who that was. For in these young years, I was two or three people, maybe even more. I was trying out many characters, to see how they felt and if they fit, and what others thought of them. I look at this picture— me seated at a school desk—and cannot guess what was going on in that head. The picture was taken by the school photographer. (My family had no camera, so the only photographs surviving are those that Ma paid a professional to take.)

It's me all right. It says so on the back, where Ma wrote my name. It's hard to read. She wrote poorly because she had little schooling in the country she came from—Austria—and none when she got here. Here's a bit of her writing, from a letter she sent me long after—the only letter of hers that I have.

My father's handwriting was better, though the only proof I have of that is his signature on the document he signed when he applied to become a citizen:

That paper was filed just three months before I was born, in 1915. Notice he spelled "Benjamin" with a final "e" instead of the usual "i." He was born in Austria, too, but not in the same village my mother came from. I'm here now, in these United States, because they emigrated to this country—Mary in 1900, and Ben in 1904. They met for the first time in New York City, when Mary's parents, Samuel and Rose Richter, took Ben in as a boarder. He was fresh off the boat and needed a place to sleep, and they needed the fifty cents a week he could pay for a bed in their apartment. Ben and Mary fell in love, got married, and had three sons. But that's getting ahead of the story.

Austria, where Ben and Mary started life, is a tiny country today. But in the nineteenth century it was a huge empire, sprawling over the heart of Europe, and run by the Emperor Franz Joseph. It boasted several great cities—Vienna, Prague, Budapest—but these were as foreign to my parents as New York.

Those two villages marked on this map are my ancestral sites, so small I couldn't find them in my atlas. I had to dig into the New York Public Library's huge collection of old maps before I located them. I never knew these names while my folks were still alive. They did not talk about their life in the old country,

and I never asked them about it. Did they wish to forget that time? Or did they think we children wouldn't be interested? If this last, then they were right. Now I think how stupid I was, how self-centered, not to be curious about the origins of my own family.

But maybe there was another reason for their silence about their past. Were they embarrassed by it? Ashamed of being greenhorns—foreigners? The heavy public pressure on immigrants to Americanize rapidly—that must have had something to do with it. These newcomers, so many people felt, are nothing and nobody. Inferior to the earlier arrivals, especially the Anglo-Saxons. So strip off your native country's culture like a ragged old coat and throw it away. Then make a new self out of Americanism. I don't think my folks were ever sure what *that* was.

Well, one part of it was certainly patriotism. And you can see, in the photo, the little patriots, my older brother Allan and me dressed up in the uniforms of World War I, with me clutching the flag. That senseless war had just ended and millions of young men were still rotting on the battlefields of Europe while we two smiled innocently into the camera. Among the countless civilians killed was my father's father—Grandfather Michael, whom I would never see—murdered at age 53 by Russian soldiers raiding his village.

It happened in 1915, the very year I was born some 5,000 miles away from where my grandfather died. I never saw my Grandmother Leah, either. She refused to leave her village, even after my grandfather was killed and the war had ended, and her children in America wrote urging her to join them and sending the ship fare. "An ungodly country," she said; she would have no part of that America. Three of her four sons had gone off without her, and one of her two daughters. Although she lived to be 94, she never saw those four children again. If they wrote to one another, not a single word of those letters remains.

When I look back at my young years in the city of Worcester, Massachusetts, I realize that all our neighbors had recently arrived from Ireland or Poland or Russia or Italy or Armenia or Greece or Sweden . . . . And today, is it any different? America is flooded by a new wave of immigrants, this time from Mexico and Colombia and Cuba and Thailand and China and Vietnam and Korea and Samoa. We all float around like a sea of weeds severed from their roots. But why feel bad about that—it is the most conspicuous advantage of being an American. You can turn your back on race and caste and class and all that had cramped and crippled your ancestors, and make a new start in this new world.

Still, I envy people who can tell me not only about their

parents and grandparents but of a long chain of family extending far, far back into time. I think, how many generations do I know, or even know of? On my mother's side, her parents, and no more. On my father's side, nothing, just the year a grandfather was killed. It gives me not a family tree, but only some twigs.

Once I heard Ben Shahn, the artist, tell how a crusty old Yankee had tried to put him down by saying her ancestors had fought at the Battle of Lexington. Shahn snapped that his had fought at the Battle of Jericho.

Nevertheless, by dint of hunting for the facts, I've learned some things that bring my European origins a little closer. My father was raised in Havrilesti, a small village in the province of Bukovina. (It's about the size of our smallest state, Rhode Island.) Today the upper part is in the west Ukraine of the Soviet Union, and the lower part is in northeast Rumania. The Carpathian mountains climb across the heavily forested countryside.

When my father was born in 1881, Austria had held Bukovina for more than a hundred years. Exactly when his ancestors settled there, I don't know. Jews from Palestine had moved in along with the Roman legions as early as the first century B.C. In the Middle Ages, when Jews were persecuted in other lands, great numbers of them began pouring into the region, from both east and west. In my father's time, many Jews of his province carried on trade in cattle, horses, and farm products. Still others made their living at handicrafts, and a smaller number as farmers.

Farming: that was what my father's family did. They lived in a wooden house with a straw roof. It had two rooms—the kitchen and a place to sleep. Leaning against the house were sheds for storing vegetables, dairy products, and farming tools.

A barn sheltered the livestock: cattle, horses, poultry. Cooking was done on the kitchen's primitive stove, which also served to heat the house. They burned wood for fuel. There was plenty of it, which is why *Bukovina* means "land of the beech trees."

Pa's family lived off what they raised in the fields, and their cattle and poultry. Any surplus was sold in the nearby small town of Gniatyn. They were Jews, these Meltzers, but their life—except for their religion—wasn't much different from the peasant life of their Ukranian neighbors. As for religion, Pa's parents were pious, and tried to instill that in their children. But from what I saw of my father, it didn't take. He never went to a synagogue, except perhaps to attend a son's Bar Mitzvah.

My father's village contained about 20 Jewish families and 400 Ukranian peasants. Under Austrian rule at that time, anti-Semitism was not open and harsh, as it was in Russia. Jews could not reach high office in government or the army, but they could live where they liked, and the trades and professions were open to them. Pa's education was limited to the public elementary school, where everything was taught in Ukranian. He worked on the family farm and was "so strong," his sister told me many years later, "that he could lift a hundred-kilo load of grain as though it were a feather." She remembered that, as the oldest son, my father played the role of protector to the other children. When the youngest child was born, my grandmother Leah was very ill for a long time, and Pa, still only a boy, took care of the infant and the household. He was very good with horses, too, she said. He used to speak to them as though they were human, and they understood and obeyed him.

In Pa's youth, hard times caused enough suffering for many Jews to decide to emigrate to America. His brother Max was the first of the family to go, mostly to avoid the military draft. Soon my father went, too. It was 1904, and he was 23.

About the life of my mother's family in the old country, I know even less. They lived in Skoryki, a village of the Galicia. Like Bukovina, Galicia was mostly farm and pasture land along the slopes of the Carpathians and the plains to the north. Since World War II, my mother's section has been part of the Ukraine in the Soviet Union. So has my father's part of Bukovina.

Ma (like Pa) was the eldest child in her family, and was born in 1888. She was the first of seven girls and two boys born to Samuel and Rose Richter. It was a marriage arranged for them by their parents. They did not meet until under the wedding canopy. Samuel, born in 1868, a year before his bride, did not know what Rose looked like until her veil was lifted moments before the ceremony. But it was a marriage that would last until death.

How Samuel earned a living in Skoryki, I do not know. It could not have been much of a living, for in 1895, thinking no doubt that in America he would find a better life, he said good-bye to Rose and their seven children and left for the New World. He was 27 years old.

I try to imagine myself in Samuel's place. Could I have done that? Break away from the home I grew up in, leave a young wife and seven little children behind, cross a strange land for a distant seaport, make the harsh voyage across the Atlantic, and start life over again in the vast chaos of New York?

I have to remind myself that taking a trip today is infinitely easier for me than it was for my grandfather nearly a hundred years ago. Travel bureaus tell me whether car, rail, ship, or plane is best, inform me of schedules and costs, describe accommodations and make reservations—whether I want to go to Boston or Bangkok. All I need is cash or a credit card.

But Grandpa knew nothing of these matters. He lived his life within the narrow limits of his village, and never had the time or money to travel beyond. Yet here he is, making the great resolve to plant roots in America. How will he go from the Old World to the New World? What season is best to travel in? Will he have trouble getting out of Austria? Where will he get the money? He is going alone, to prepare the way for the family to follow. How will they live while he is gone?

He crossed the Atlantic in steerage. That was the cheapest class on the steamship. He slept in a compartment way below decks that held about 300 immigrants. The berths, in two tiers, were six feet, two inches long, with a two-and-a-half-foot space above each berth. The iron framework held a mattress and a pillow stuffed with straw or seaweed. His blanket was so flimsy that he had to sleep in his clothing to keep warm. The voyage lasted 16 days, but the stewards never cleaned his berth. There was no room for hand baggage. The few things he had carried from home—a pot, a teakettle, an embroidered pillowcase Rose had made for him—he kept in his berth. (The floor was forbidden.) He had no closet or hooks; everything he was not wearing had to be piled on the narrow berth. Even the eating utensils the shipping line supplied had to be tucked under the mattress.

No dining room was provided. Samuel lined up with the other passengers for his food and ate it in his berth. There were no waste barrels or sickness cans; the steerage floor was always damp and filthy and the air stank sickeningly. And the food? A chunk of white bread that tasted like chalk and a smelly herring. (He would not take the nonkosher meat or soup.) After two days of that diet, he dug into the hardtack and the rocklike farmer cheese he had been advised to stow into his pack. When a storm came up their fourth day out, he didn't need food. He had plenty to give up as the boat rocked and shook.

Privacy was for the aristocrats on the upper decks. Down

below, the men, women, and children were all mixed together. A shy man, Samuel turned his glance away when his neighbors took off their clothing. He stayed in what he wore the day he boarded ship.

They all suffered for lack of water. Just one small cup was handed out each evening, and it had to do for 24 hours. Samuel learned you could get more of it for money, but he couldn't spare a penny. By evening, he often burned with thirst, and couldn't hoard the cupful handed to him. After a week at sea, his energy gone, his spirits low, he wondered why he had done this crazy thing. He lay on his bunk in a stupor. When his stomach churned and he needed the toilet, he had to wait in a long line. There were only eight toilets and eight washbasins for about 250 women and children, and the same ratio for the men. When he finally got in, the toilet seats were wet and water stood inches deep on the floor. Since breakfast was at seven, Samuel had to get up by five or even earlier to make it into the washroom on time. After a few days of that, he gave up trying to stay clean. There was no bathtub or shower, and if he stayed at a washbasin for more than a few seconds, a growl of anger went up from the line behind him.

But when his ship steamed into New York harbor, he felt the heavy blanket of oppression lift. He drank in the rich green of Staten Island and the soft blue of sky and sea, the bustle of the boats hurrying across the bay and those floating many-windowed palaces he learned were ferries.

When Samuel arrived in 1895, the Old Castle Garden receiving station for immigrants had been replaced only three years before by a new station on Ellis Island. It was a tiny blob of mud and sand lying in a shallow of the harbor, enlarged a bit by landfill. The main building was a two-story structure that looked like a big seaside hotel.

The immigrants on Samuel's ship were taken off in small boats, each group numbered and lettered so that when they stepped ashore the man with the pen, who asked questions, could match them against the passenger list. Samuel waited in a little stall with the others in his group, all huddled together, sweating in fear and anxiety. Would they be let in or turned back?

He answered the questions satisfactorily, the doctor gave him a clean bill of health, and he was admitted. His ordeal was over. A few minutes later he was eating his first decent meal in weeks in a big waiting room. Then the ferry carried Samuel to Battery Park at the tip of Manhattan.

America! America! Here I am!

"Better They Don't End Up in a Sweatshop, Too"

Sweatshop

The Granger Collection

Culver
Pictures

The Lower East Side

Culver Pictures

New York—and Skoryki. No two worlds could have been more stunningly different. The muddy village of old Austria, and the towering steel of New York into which Samuel had dropped. The tall buildings, the gas and electric lamps that turned night into day, the horsecars and trolleys, the elevated trains thundering overhead. On the streets, blacks, Chinese, Italians, Irish, a host of nationalities he had never seen before. He wanted to speak to them, to know what they thought, how they differed from the people he had grown up with. But their languages he could not understand, and his shyness was too high a hurdle to leap.

He headed for the Lower East Side. There he knew he would see and be with Jews. From the Battery to that neighborhood wasn't far to go. His ears took in the sweet familiar sound of Yiddish, and his eyes the signboards swinging their messages in Yiddish or English or Russian. Hurry, scurry, hustle, bustle. Getting through these crowded streets was a happy torment. Here all was strange, yet somehow familiar, too. The passersby, even the street peddlers, were better dressed than in Skoryki.

They wore hats, not caps, even stiff collars and neckties. The women, too, sported hats or bonnets. Suddenly Samuel realized some of the people he passed were smiling at him. Did they know him? No, that couldn't be. Then he noticed one of them nudge another and say in Yiddish, "There goes a greener!" He understood. He was the newcomer, the inexperienced one to be pitied and maybe scorned. They, of course, were not. Maybe they came only yesterday, but already they think they're Americanized.

He found a place to live on the Lower East Side, boarding with an immigrant family in a tenement flat. There were three other boarders, all jammed into two rooms. For 50 cents a day he got bed, breakfast and dinner. Soon he landed a job, learning the tailoring trade in a garment factory, sewing men's pants. The boss advanced him a down payment on a sewing machine, the rest of the money to be taken weekly out of his pay. He lugged the machine to work on his back every day. His pay was $5 a week, for a 14-hour day.

Slowly Samuel made a few friends—another boarder, a shop-mate, a waiter in the kosher restaurant. But he still felt alone. Day and night, he thought of Rose and the children. From his heart a painful aching spread through his whole body, to his very fingers and toes. It was the desolation of the uprooted. He had not left home because he hated his village. No, he loved the place, and still did, though now he could see how much it lacked. Going away was like ripping out a piece of his soul.

Two years later, he went back home. He stayed for two years, and again saw how hopeless it was in Skoryki. Maybe, he told Rose, just maybe, if our Mary joins me in New York, as soon as I can save the money to send for her ship fare, then the two of us together could earn enough to bring you all over.

So they said good-bye once more, and back he went. A year

later, in 1900, my mother Mary joined him. She was 12 then. There was no room for her where Samuel boarded, so she boarded nearby with a family that only took in girls. One of them steered her to a job in a small ladies' coat shop. Mary had never been inside a factory of any kind. This was a low, crowded room in a big loft building. As she came through the door she was almost overwhelmed by the thick close air, smelling of sweat and hot with steam. The room was alive with the ceaseless whir of machines. The workers clumped in teams of three, the operator sitting hunched over his sewing machine, his foot on the treadle in ceaseless motion, the baster standing just behind, at a table, and the finisher working close between them. On the table she saw 20 coats piled high: that was their quota, the day's work that must be finished by the time they left the shop, often 15 hours after they entered.

She saw no overseer on the floor. The teams seemed to drive themselves to make the day's wages. The swiftest of them set the pace and the others rushed to catch up. If one felt sick or exhausted, the others put on the pressure. Mary knew how to sew from earliest childhood, and she quickly fitted in. She had endless stores of energy and a boundless determination to do things right and do them rapidly. The boss was soon calling her "my darling, a real gift from heaven." But to her team, she was a threat. "To keep up with her, you got to kill yourself," they said. She had been there a few weeks when a truant officer came in to look for children who were illegally out of school. (You had to be 16 to work.) Mary was prepared: she pulled out a certificate on which Samuel had sworn that she was 16. She knew, too, that if the officer was suspicious, the boss was ready to bribe him.

Low as their pay was in the sweatshops, Mary and Samuel managed to save enough in less than three years to buy passage for the whole family to come over. Samuel had prepared for the arrival of Rose and their big brood—Gussie, Harry, Eva, the twins Anna and Dora, and the littlest, Sally. With Mary, they moved into a big red brick tenement house on the Lower East Side, at 215 East 4th Street.

The tenement was arranged in the shape of a dumbbell. Four apartments on a floor, two at each end of a narrow corridor. Samuel had rented a front apartment. There was a kitchen, a parlor, and two bedrooms. One of the bedrooms was always rented to a boarder. To bed Samuel's big family, all the other rooms had to be turned into sleeping quarters when night came. The children slept on folding cots or on an arrangement of chairs. But it didn't seem cramped to Rose. Not after their tiny house in Skoryki. And here there was a toilet! And running water! No more walking to the outhouse in all kinds of weather, or hauling buckets of water from the well. True, the toilet and the sink were in the hallway, and had to meet the needs of four large families. But it made the hall a busy place, where you met neighbors when they had a pitcher to fill for drinking water, or a pot for cooking. And usually there was a mother waiting to fill a tub for her children's baths.

Rose liked having the water so handy, but just as important was the chance to talk, or listen. "It's a regular talking newspaper out there," Samuel would snort. But Rose enjoyed passing the gossip around—who was getting married, who expecting a baby, who having a *bris*, who a Bar Mitzvah, who falling sick, who dying. Privacy in such a home? Impossible! But was that so bad?

Here, in the tenement, where 24 families lived, were dozens of lives. Immigrants all, but behind every door, a different story, a separate life. One wounded and hopeless, beaten down by the harsh competition for work and bread; another cheerful, sunny, filled with expectation. A Yiddish poet in this flat, a coarse ignoramus in that one; parents whose children had become thieves and prostitutes, and parents whose children were scholars and hard workers. Parents whose children had deserted them, and children who had left their parents behind in the old country. The joyous eyes of a dreamy young girl, the blank stare of an exhausted young worker. All these Rose saw within the high walls of her tenement house.

They settled in with a few chairs, a kitchen table, dishes and cooking things, a bed for Samuel and Rose, cots for the children. Little by little, they added a soft chair, a sofa, curtains, the fixings needed to make the place livable.

The first thing on my grandparents' mind was to get the children into school. The older ones had had some Jewish training in Skoryki, nothing more. Now they would start "to become Americans," and learn it all in that strange tongue, English. They began in a public school just around the corner. It was a special class, for beginners in English between the ages of 6 and 15, each desk fitted out with pencil box, writing pad, and a colored blotter. It was "see-a-cat," "hear-a-dog-bark," "look-at-the-hen" until the words began to make sense and they were thinking and seeing and feeling in the new language. When they got stuck, the teacher let them help each other with a word in Yiddish.

"Learn, learn, learn!" Grandpa kept saying. "You got to study hard to get anywhere in this America!" And sometimes, home late, eating the warmed-over supper with Rose, the table scattered with schoolbooks, he would mutter, "Better they don't end up in a sweatshop, too."

But they did.

The City
of Three-Deckers

Ma and Pa

Our Three-Decker

Rotterdam was the port in Holland that my father sailed from. And the ship he boarded was called *The Rotterdam*. I always knew his name as Benjamin, but in Bukovina it was Peretz. He must have made it Benjamin—the first step to Americanization!—after he arrived at Ellis Island. That was on August 12, 1904. He was 23.

He found a place to live, boarding in my grandfather Samuel's apartment, and as I said, that was how he met my mother. Mary was a pretty girl of 16, a few inches under his 5 feet 5. She had thick dark hair piled high, large brown eyes, a full figure. Lively and outspoken, she must have charmed the shy, quiet Benjamin. He had wavy brown hair, gray eyes, a very white skin, and the sturdy build of a farmer. They were very different in nature. Mary loved to dance and went wherever the chance offered. But Ben never dared venture on the floor. At first, when they were courting, she would leave him to go out with her friends to dance. But when she saw how it upset him to see her go off without him, she gave up dancing.

They married, and in 1911, had their first child, Aaron. Later he changed his name to Allan. Working in a bedspring factory, Ben saw little hope of bettering his prospects in New York. Then a cousin, who was living in Boston, wrote that Worcester, a town in Massachusetts, needed window cleaners, a trade that required almost no training. So Ben and Mary with their infant son moved to Worcester. You needed little capital to obtain the tools of that trade: a squeegee, a pole, a pail, a chamois cloth, a safety belt, and a telephone with which to take orders. The new enterprise was cheaply launched. Ben knew he would never get rich. But free of sweatshops, he would at least be his own boss.

He found a place for them to live on the east side of Worcester—the immigrant and working-class district. It was an apartment in a three-tenement house at 2 Chapin Street. One block long, the street perched upon one of the town's many steep hills. To Ben and Mary, their apartment, taking up a whole floor, was a palace. Three bedrooms, a big kitchen, their own bathroom, a parlor, a porch! Windows in front, in back, on both sides! Fresh air coming in from all directions! Sunlight! And quiet, heavenly quiet . . . All this, after years on the Lower East Side, one of the most crowded slums in the world.

To absorb the rapidly expanding working class of these New England towns, someone had dreamed up the three-decker design. Land was plentiful; there was no need to jam the cheap wooden houses together. In the small space between, neighbors planted grass and trees and even flowers. Across the street was the school I'd go to, Union Hill Grammar. And just beyond, taking up many acres on the hill, was Worcester Academy. The old prep school catered to upper-class boys from all across the country. Behind its walls were ivy-covered red brick dormitories and classrooms, gym and library, theater and dining hall, joined by paved walks that laced the deep green lawns. The place seemed so patrician to me that I hardly dared venture through the gates. But my father did, often and regularly. He cleaned the Academy's windows.

On May 8, 1915, I was born in City Hospital. When I was about three, we moved from Chapin Street to the foot of the hill, to 52 Vale Street, another three-decker on a street of three-deckers. (There were so many thousands of these buildings that Worcester was called "the City of Three-Deckers.") At least half the city lived in them when I was born. This time we had the top floor, with a porch or "piazza," as we called it, where you could read or sun yourself or snooze in a hammock. The rent was $15 a month.

When I was a child, rambling up our dirt street, past the great open meadows, I found a big rock planted deep in the earth. Carved on its face was the thrilling news that Jonas Rice, the first permanent settler of Worcester, had built his log cabin right here on my street! That had been 1713, and for over a year, he was the only dweller in that wilderness of swamps and woods. Then his brother joined him, and, in a few years, settlers built many more cabins.

Sitting on Jonas's rock, I could imagine the wolves howling in the night and hear the bloodcurdling shrieks of the bands of Nipmuck Indians who burned cabins and attacked settlements which threatened their hunting and planting grounds. Only a few years before Jonas arrived, Diggory Sargent's cabin on Union Hill (called *Sagatabscot* by the Indians) had been raided, and Diggory and his wife killed. Two of their children, taken by the Indians, remained with them and adopted their ways. But Jonas Rice stayed fast, and in 1722, Worcester officially became a town. It was named after the city in England where Oliver Cromwell defeated the forces of Charles II in 1651. Pronounced "Wooster," it means "war-castle."

A few years more, and Worcester became the seat of the new county of the same name. Some people didn't appreciate the upgrading. County seats were the site of court sessions, and in those days, the gathering of judges and plaintiffs and defendants meant a holiday. Wrestling, fighting, horse-racing, and boozing took over, with the farmer-jockeys racing wildly down Main Street. Too raucous a time for the quieter souls.

Many of them remembered the days when wolves and rattlesnakes were so numerous you won a bounty for killing them. Bears and wildcats were common. In hundreds of lakes and streams, you could fish for trout and bass, perch and pickerel. The noise of hammer and saw at work on new cabins startled from their nests flocks of wild pigeons, ducks, quail, partridge, and turkey.

These I could no longer see, of course, but surely the Indians had left something of their lives? Old Jonas Rice's rock was in an empty lot. With a pointed stick, I dug here and there beneath the long grass, looking for signs of a disappeared people. But I never did find a stone tool, an arrowhead, a tomahawk, or even a bit of broken pottery. Then one day it dawned on me that echoes of Indian voices were all around me. The place names I had taken for granted—Quinsigamond, Tatnuck, Packachoag, Wachuset, Asnebumskit—were the beautiful names Indians gave to the lakes, streams, and hills they loved so much.

One of my earliest memories of schooldays is linked to the Indians. I was in the third grade of Union Hill Grammar School when the teacher, Miss Joyce, staged a short play about how the Pilgrims and the Indians came to celebrate the first Thanksgiving in the New World. She cast me as Chief Massasoit. We had read about the sad time the Pilgrims had, when half their company died at Plymouth in that first winter in Massachusetts. Then the Indians, who had been watching the newcomers struggle to get a foothold, came into the settlement, exchanged gifts, and made a peace treaty. Dressed like an Indian in a costume my mother made from a picture Miss Joyce sent home, and with a great flourish of chicken feathers sweeping from my head down my back to the floor, I did my regal best to overawe the Pilgrims and the audience as I signed the peace treaty. Then with my band of Indians, we walked noiselessly off stage, heel-and-toe, in Indian-style that we practiced for hours. But what I remember best is that we learned that the Indians taught the Pilgrims their native ways of fishing and farming. When and how to trap and catch fish. How and when to plant corn in hill rows, using fish for fertilizer. Without those lessons, said Miss Joyce, the Pilgrims might all have died. It was my first inkling that whites didn't know it all. They had much to learn from others. But not until years later did I find out—and write about—how whites repaid Indians in blood and the theft of their land.

I started at Union Hill School when I was five. I climbed up the steep slope of Dorchester Street, clinging to my brother Allan's hand. He was going on nine then, and considered me a nuisance. But Ma said, "Take him there!" and so he handed me over to Miss Melaven, the kindergarten teacher, and hastily backed away. But I let up a howl, mixed of fear of the unknown, and grief at the loss of my freedom. I cried piteously until the teacher waved Allan out. Then I quickly subsided, for I took to school as though born to learn.

The first thing I remember learning was a merry little tune we sang every morning as Miss Melaven called us to order, ceremoniously blew her silver whistle, and gave us the downbeat.

> Good morning to you, good morning to you,
> We're all in our places with sunshiny faces,
> Oh this is the way, to start a new day!

Perhaps it was the next year, in the first grade, that Miss Riley tried to lead us gently into the ways of hygiene. Since some of us were foreign-born, and most of us were the children of immigrants, the school assumed that the benighted countries we sprang from didn't know much about personal cleanliness. Sitting in our seats, while pantomiming the routines, we sang,

> *This is the way we brush our teeth, brush our teeth,*
> > *brush our teeth,*
> *This is the way we brush our teeth*
> *So early in the morning!*

And on into the next routine: "This is the way we wash our hands," and finally, "This is the way we comb our hair." Easily memorized, the messages were carried home. To make sure we practiced what was preached, Miss Riley would now and then inspect each pupil's head of hair, and if lice were visible, it meant fierce scrubbing with harsh soap.

I loved everything about that school—learning to read, to write, to add and subtract, to take the first stumbling steps toward finding out where I was in my small world and what was going on in it.

I won some honor for spelling in that school. It came naturally to me. I didn't need painful drilling or memorizing. If I came across a new word it was almost instinctive that I would spell it correctly—though sometimes I didn't realize I was mispro-ouncing it in my head until I heard someone say it properly. (*Misled*, for instance. It was "mizzled" to me for an awfully long time.) Teachers used spelling bees to encourage us in that skill. I'd win first prize, then go on to sweep the school prize, and once the citywide competition. There were national spelling bees in those days, but I was never sent to compete in those.

At Union Hill, all our teachers were Irish. Their ancestors

had come from the Emerald Isle in the 1820s to help construct the local Blackstone Canal. In the 1830s they built the Boston and Worcester Railroad. With the potato famine of the 1840s in Ireland, the New England towns became "full of Irish," as the writer Ralph Waldo Emerson noted. They were almost completely shunned by the old-time Yankees who considered these new immigrants hardly members of the human race. Only the most menial jobs were open to them. But gradually they moved on up. In 1895 Worcester elected its first Irish-Catholic mayor, Philip O'Connell. And now, in my childhood, it was the Irish who largely staffed the public schools. A change our Yankee second President, John Adams, would never have predicted. When he was fresh out of Harvard, in 1755, he spent three years teaching in Worcester, in a one-room school on Court Hill.

My teachers were not only all Irish, but all of them were women, and all of them were single. Local rules didn't permit female teachers to be married, and demanded a strict code of behavior. Step out of line even an inch, and they were fired. But it didn't limit what they could do to the children. In one of Allan's classes, a girl came into the room with just a dab of face-powder on her cheek. Miss McDonald grabbed her by the hair, dragged her to the sink, and scrubbed it off, calling her a whore. The kids hated that teacher for her violent reactions. One Friday evening, Allan and Jack, a pal of his, decided to call Miss McDonald on the phone. Dropping his voice to what he hoped was a low rumble, Allan asked the woman who answered: "Is this Miss McDonald?" "Yes," she replied, and leaning into the mouthpiece, the two kids screamed, "Screw you, Miss McDonald!" then hung up and fled outdoors.

That was a defiant gesture I never would have made. Which is perhaps why Allan scornfully called me the goody-goody. He was a model for misbehavior, the despair of Ma and Pa. One time at table, they accused him of doing somthing wrong, and he answered truthfully that *he* hadn't done it; I had. Whereupon Pa smacked him hard, yelling, "So he's learning from you, you bum!"

I didn't learn much from him. Only what not to do. Wherever I followed him in school, the teachers eyed me suspiciously until I proved myself "safe." Allan was smaller than most kids of his age, and was made to wear eyeglasses very early because his vision was so poor. Glasses were neither common nor fashionable in those times, and the other kids tagged him "Four-eyes." On top of that, he was naturally left-handed. This was considered an appalling handicap, so terrible it could blight a youngster's life. So the schools forced him to switch to the right, a real nightmare for him.

He had found out he was bright, very bright, almost as soon as he started school. He knew it, and he didn't hesitate to let you know it, too. In one of his classes, the teacher staged a Nativity play for the Christmas season. As she looked about the room to cast the parts, she fastened on Allan and said, "You'll play the First Wise Man." And turning to the other children she added, "He thinks he's so smart he should play all three Wise Men." They laughed.

During a sixth-grade art class one day, Miss Moran handed out a nice rag paper so that pupils could work with watercolors. Allan was nervous at the task, knowing his right hand couldn't control the running colors, and his sweaty hands smudged the paper badly. Leaning over his shoulder, Miss Moran spotted the mess. "Filthy little pig!" she said, and held up the smudged sheet for all to see.

With nearly four years separating us, we didn't play together or share friends. Smart-ass kid that he was, he wanted desperately to be accepted by the bigger boys in class. After school, he chose the toughest kids in the neighborhood to hang out with. They didn't care for school, so neither did he. He sassed the teachers and broke most of the rules. Suspended twice, he became the constant worry of Ma and Pa. They knew how intelligent he was, and they hoped that somehow they would be able to send their first-born son to college. With that big mouth, they used to say smilingly, you can be a fine lawyer some day. No one on either side of our family had yet gone to college. It was their dream that Allan would make it. (He did, but not in the academic way; he became a success in the world of business.)

He reached Classical, the Worcester high school designed to prepare students for college. In his first year there, he missed class for a while, recovering from a leg broken during a neighborhood football game. When he got back to school, he didn't work hard to catch up in math, and Mr. Howland gave him a "D warning." That meant he had to stay in after school each day, and study under supervision. Mr. Howland came up behind him one afternoon, and saw that Allan was reading a novel, hidden between the pages of the math text propped up on his desk. He snatched it away and said angrily, "Meltzer, you're a thief!" Shocked by such a charge, Allan said, "What do you mean by that?" The teacher replied, "You're stealing the school's time!" Allan gave Mr. Howland a shove. The teacher fell over a chair and Allan ran out of the room. Next day, when he entered the school, the principal, Mr. Fenner, was waiting for him. "Get out!" he yelled. "You're expelled!"

For a while, my brother pretended to go to school each day, leaving at the right hour in the morning and coming back each afternoon. He had been suspended from other schools, to the bitter disappointment and anger of Ma and Pa. He feared what they would say and do now. Finally, unable to go on with the charade, and with thirty cents in his pocket, he ran away from home. He was 14. He hitchhiked to New York, got work as an errand boy in the garment district, and lived in a room up in the Bronx. Ma and Pa were frantic. Where was he? Sick? Injured? Dead? He left no word, never telephoned or wrote. The police put out an alarm, but no one found him.

A year later, too lonely in the strange city, he returned home. My mother opened the door one day to find him standing there. She fainted dead away.

A Hunger for Words

Krazy Kat,
Offissa Pup,
and Ignatz Mouse

Reprinted with special permission of King Features Syndicate

I don't know when I fell in love with the printed word. How did I learn to read? I can't remember. I could not read, and then one day I *could* read. We had no books at home. Ma and Pa had neither the money to buy nor the time to read them. No one had read to them when they were little, and they did not think of doing that with me. It must have been in school that the reading began. And then it was the Little Red Hen primers, a dull diet!

But there were other books, hundreds of years old, which were far more imaginative. Early on, a teacher gave me *The Arabian Nights* to read. It was a big, handsome book, with large type and broad white margins, and magnificently colored pictures. Fairy tales, reaching me from far-off Eastern lands—Arabia, Persia, Syria, Egypt, India, Mesopotamia. Enchanted realms ruled by the great Haroun al Raschid, Caliph of Bagdad, Commander of the Faithful. The stories were spun out to a cruel Sultan for a thousand and one nights by the lovely princess Scheherazade. Page by page, her tales carried me into strange lost cities. Here I first met Ali Baba and the Forty Thieves, Sinbad the Sailor, Aladdin and his wonderful Lamp. The tales pumped fresh blood into my veins and made me eager to search out the unpredictable wonders of the world.

Later, another teacher loaned me *Gulliver's Travels*, in an edition that contained only the first two parts, the voyages to Lilliput and Brobdingnag. To me it was a thrilling picture of life at sea, this personal tale of Lemuel Gulliver, the Irishman who floats through a world of pygmies and giants. What lay underneath—the mockery of politicans, of kings and queens, of crimes and vices, of petty quarrels between nations—I hardly grasped at the time. It was Jonathan Swift's gift as a storyteller that held me, the sheer adventure that I relished.

It must have been the desire for more books like these that led me to the public library. One Saturday morning, I found myself downtown, on Elm Street, a long way from our neighborhood, looking up at a tall building of dark red stone. I climbed the high steps and walked into a world I would never leave. Off the main hallways were the treasures I was hunting for. Dozens, hundreds, thousands of books packed into shelves running along the wall, reaching from the floor far higher than my eager fingertips could stretch.

Hungry for the printed word, my appetite was insatiable. I started at one wall of the children's room and worked my way around to the last. There was a limit to the number of books you could borrow. But after a few weeks, when the librarian saw that I returned every Saturday morning with the books I had taken the previous week, she ignored the rules and let me borrow as many as my arms could hold.

At first the librarian would suggest a title or an author to me. But she soon realized that mine was a fundamental hunger. I was like some insect nibbling words to appease an instinctive craving. So she let me alone, waiting for a time when I would begin to see connections between books, and ask for her help. But for a long while, I yanked books off shelves at random, sampling everything.

My grammar school had no library, and the new junior high put so much money into building and equipment that it left little for books. That library was almost as bare of books as was my home. So I built my own library. Cheap paperbacks— a dime each—they were my first purchase. Horatio Alger! *There* was a writer who knew what I wanted. Plenty of exciting adventures, one piled atop another, and plenty of dialogue. His stories had but one pattern. The hero is a poor but honest lad, and usually an orphan. After a string of adventures that reveal many sides of city life, the hero saves the life of a rich man's daughter. Her grateful father gives our hero a job in his business and the climb from rags to riches is on its way. The young hero always behaves well, quietly displays strength of character, and proves to be lucky, a gift that comes only to those who deserve it.

Alger, graduate of Harvard's Divinity School, began his long and productive writing career just after the Civil War. Though he died some 15 years before my birth, we still read his stories and loved them. *Sink or Swim, Strive and Succeed, Wait and Hope, Try and Trust, Rough and Ready*—these books we swapped among us until they fell apart.

Alger's heroes were not just fictional. The America of his time had many real Alger-like heroes. Daniel Webster: from saloon-keeper's son to Senator; James A. Garfield: from canal boy to President; Cornelius Vanderbilt: from farm boy to the richest man in the world. Henry Ford, A. T. Stewart, Joseph Pulitzer, and dozens more in a colorful pantheon of success-gods. What Alger said to us was that we too, the immigrant children on the street, could win fame and fortune one day. It didn't bother me that all those books read alike. I'm sure I didn't realize it then.

As Alger grew old and tired, his place as king of the dime novels was taken by a much younger rival, Edward Stratemeyer. He became the greatest producer of boy's books in the country. So much so that his powers overflowed into a syndicate he built which employed many hack writers to turn his three-page outlines into 200-page books. (He died when I was in high school, but his syndicate carries on right down to this day, manufacturing many series, such as Nancy Drew and the Hardy Boys, that sell in the multimillions.) His dime novels starring Nick Carter, the master detective, were in as great demand on our block as the Alger stories. Think of the alluring titles: *Nick Carter Among the Poisoners . . . Among the Hotel Thieves . . .*

An altogether different delight came from the Frank Merriwell series. The pulp writer Gilbert Patten turned these out under the name of Burt L. Standish. They featured Frank and, later, his young brother Dick, both students at Yale. I lived in a fantasy of going to Yale some day, strolling under the great trees on the beautiful campus, watching our football and baseball teams battling Harvard, joking with my chums in the dorms, entertaining beautiful girls down from Wellesley or Radcliffe on weekends. That the Merriwell bunch were all WASPs, with not a Jew in sight, never occurred to me. The writing anticipated the *Time* magazine style created not long after. Everybody's name was preceded by an identifying tag: "excitable Harry Rattleton," "lumbering Bart Hodge," "handsome Dick Merriwell." Again, formula books, but who cared.

Much tamer, because it was for much younger readers, was the Bobbsey Twin series I came across at the right age. They were two pairs of twins, the Bobbseys, aged four to eight. I shared their calm life at home, in school, at the seashore, and on the ranch.

Although I never was a skilled baseball player or an ardent fan, I enjoyed the Baseball Joe series. I followed Joe through Yale (the dream school again) and on into the minor leagues, the big leagues, the World Series, and finally around the world on tour.

These paperbacks were in and out of my room quickly, exchanged for others as soon as I'd devoured them. Meanwhile, every day, I read the comic strips—the "funnies," we called them—in the newspaper. Weekdays they were plain black-and-white, then on Sunday they bloomed into full-pagers, in bright color. *Gasoline Alley* I remember because it was like a novel: the people in it grew up and grew old, they weren't fixed at the same stage in every strip. I could follow the destiny of Skeezix, the boy who had been left on Uncle Walt's doorstep as a baby. His adventures were never wild or fantastic, they were more like our own, and the family was gentle and warmhearted and reassuring.

Very different were *The Katzenjammer Kids*, two boys rollicking in slapstick comedy, mischievous types a bit like Tom Sawyer. Strangest of all was *Krazy Kat,* a strip featuring a dog named Offissa Pup, Krazy Kat herself (or himself—you couldn't be sure), and Ignatz Mouse. Flouting the laws of nature, the dog loved the cat and the cat loved the mouse. But Ignatz, the mouse, loved nobody. Offissa Pup was always chasing madly after Krazy Kat while Ignatz heaved bricks at both of them from the sidelines. I'm not sure what I was laughing at, but I never missed that strip.

The only hardcover book I saw in our three-decker house was stuffed into a neighbor's bric-a-brac shelf. The Reeds, who lived on the first floor of our three-decker, had acquired a stout one-volume medical encyclopedia. Dipping into it one day, when bored with the adult talk around me, I came across detailed illustrations of the human anatomy. I scanned them hastily and guiltily, put the book back as casually as I'd return the milk to the icebox. The next day, I found an excuse to drop in on the Reeds. I waited till no one else was in the parlor, then took the book off the shelf and studied the anatomy with great care, astonished and disturbed, too, at the differences between male and female.

Sex was a great mystery to me. I never asked Ma or Pa about it. It was something you discussed with your friends, not with grown-ups. I kept quiet about it because I didn't want to admit that it bothered me. Besides, what adult would answer my questions? The little I knew about it came from the street-corner experts. One of them put flesh on the medical drawings by showing me a saucer-eyed young woman in silken underwear posing provocatively on the cover of a pocket-sized magazine. He flipped the pages to reveal dozens of such girls in various stages of undress. Suddenly I felt I knew all about it, although I didn't know how you did it, or what to do about it. It would be a while before I learned that.

At Union Hill school, I was so fascinated by a tiny girl that I often followed her home at a safe distance, and waited patiently outside for hours in hope of glimpsing her again. Gertrude her name was, a name that seemed to me the most beautiful name for a girl, a name that I murmured quietly to myself. Did she ever suspect how secretly I suffered for her? She acted unaware of my existence, even when I kept staring at her in class and on the playground. By the time I was ten, girls and boys mixed a little. On Saturday afternoons, we went to parties in the girls' homes, chiefly to giggle and tease and play kissing games. No sooner would I return home, than the phone would start ringing. It was Helen asking, "What do you think of Sylvia?" Or Freddy wanting to know, "Did you get anywhere with

Rachel?" Disgusted, Ma would yell, "Get off the phone!"

Leaving Union Hill school at age 12 meant a great change. Grafton Street Junior High was at the other, the lower end of Dorchester Street, still an easy walk from home. It was a huge new brick building, drawing its students from several neighborhoods. After the coziness of grammar school, these dozens of rooms and miles of corridors swarming with boys and girls I had never seen before were intimidating.

The studies I was used to—English, history, geography, science, math—were no problem, but now I had to take shop courses every term. First it was woodworking, then printing, then sheet-metal and home mechanics and mechanical drawing. I got by, but shakily. I never developed the confidence to work well with my hands. Except for printing. The smell of the ink, and the different kinds of paper, the clank of the handpress, the roar of the power press, delighted me. I loved the dazzling array of typefaces, the speed and accuracy with which I could set something with the composing stick, making up a page on the printer's stone, preparing the press and running off the proofs, and seeing the handsome result on a gleaming white sheet.

The instructor, a middle-aged man who once worked in a newspaper plant, was proud of his craft. He told us how Ben Franklin had made his living as a printer, and that Mark Twain had become an apprentice printer at 13, the very age all of us boys were. Yes, boys—for none of these craft classes were open to the girls. Nursing and home management, cooking and sewing—that was for them. No one thought anything wrong with it.

In junior high I lost some of my shyness. Getting mostly A's and B's, even in Latin and French, made me feel good. Then an eye examination revealed that I needed to wear glasses, not just for reading, but all the time. It was a blow. How would I do with girls now? It was like starting out on an important race with a bad handicap. But when I fixed a greedy eye on Ingrid, a handsome blonde, and sensed her response, I stopped worrying about glasses.

We began meeting after school, and I'd walk her home. She lived some distance from me. On the way, we went by an abandoned quarry. One afternoon, weeks after the walks began, she said, "Let's see if anything's growing down there." We climbed down the tumbled rocks. I helped Ingrid keep her balance, now taking her hand, now putting an arm around her waist. At the bottom, we turned to each other and as though nothing else had ever been on our minds, embraced. We clung together, then kissed. Neither of us seemed to know how. With mouths closed and lips tight, we just pushed hard, making pounds of pressure register our feeling. Up top someone yelled, "Hey, look at this!" and three small boys scampered along the quarry's rim, jeering at us. We pulled apart and slowly climbed up. We walked to her house in silence, and I left. The next day, in class, we smiled at each other. But we never went back to the quarry, and, after a while, I stopped walking her home.

Why? I'm not sure. But I was learning how easy it was to fall in love with almost any girl. After Ingrid there was Theresa, then Sarah, and then Stella. Nothing went much further than that time in the quarry. Except with Stella. She was a large round girl, placid, and would stare at me with her unblinking blue eyes, listening to my chatter, saying nothing in return, waiting, waiting—for what? One day, leaving school with her, I surprised myself by saying, "Let's stop at my house for a few minutes." I gave no reason why, and she asked for none. My heart began to race when she nodded. I knew that afternoon no one would be home. Maybe, alone, something would happen. I prayed no neighbor would see us enter. Inside the apartment,

I steered her straight to my bedroom. We stood by the bed, and kissed. I was somewhat better at it now, and Stella more than matched me. Then we lay on the bed, hugging hard enough, it seemed, to print each body on the other. All the while saying nothing, only sighing and gasping and groaning. I don't know how long it went on, but the thought suddenly flashed into my head that my mother might come in any minute. Terrified, I leaped up and pulled Stella out of the house, my legs trembling so I could hardly stand. You're crazy to take such chances, I told myself. I never asked Stella to try it again.

The Dump
and the Candy Store

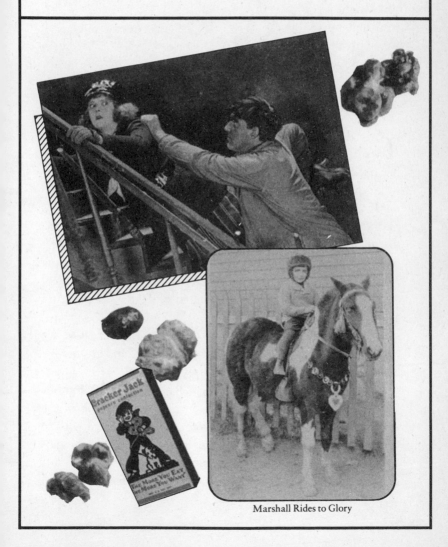

Marshall Rides to Glory

The mystery of girls loomed large in my thoughts and dreams, but it did not take up all my time. School ate up a third of my waking hours; that still left time for fun and work. I worked hard, and played hard. There were plenty of places to play, and plenty of things to do. The corner candy store, the public parks, the open fields, Lake Quinsigamond with its seven-mile sheet of clean water and along its shore tennis courts and sandy beach and a float with a diving board. White City, too, a dazzling amusement park, and vaudeville theaters and movie houses. And always the streets.

Unlike the kids who grew up in the huge crowded cities, we had space, light, air. There was plenty of open land around us: grassy lots between some of the houses along Vale Street, a huge stretch of field and orchard sloping steeply upward behind our house, and in back of the houses on the opposite side of the street, a vast, marshy meadow called Cheney's Field. In the winter, after a freezing rain, Cheney's became sheeted ice, glorious for skating and hockey. In good weather we played football and baseball there. On the hilly meadow, people had planted fruit trees and potato patches. We swiped apples and spuds and roasted them over small fires hidden in the hollows.

Even with that much space, we played on the street, too. Parents did nothing to stop us, for the traffic was so minor, there was little risk. So we played as we pleased. There were a dozen variations on games with ball and bat. We played marbles, spun tops, flew kites, kicked the can, leapfrogged fire hydrants and one another, pitched pennies, and shot crap. We played king of the mountain, follow the leader, ringelevio, prisoner's base. None of these games needed equipment. When a game called for that, we improvised. A broom handle and rubber ball did for baseball, with rocks, hats, or lampposts for bases. Stuffed bags were footballs, broken baby carriages were turned into wagons, barrel staves into skis, abandoned bicycle wheels into hoops, metal garbage covers into sleds.

We made up our own rules for any game we played. The loudest voice often decided what was fair and foul and meted out the punishment for kids who broke the rules. Mostly we played after school, and before dark. Teachers disappeared, parents were indoors or at work, we were free. I don't remember anyone's mother or father coming out to watch us play. So long as we didn't abandon younger brothers or sisters, or get hurt, they left us alone.

A good time was what we wanted. Mostly, it had to be free. Few of the families on our side of town earned enough to buy fun. I never had an allowance. I don't think I even knew that word. If what you wanted cost money, you usually had to earn it yourself. Oh, a nickel or a dime could be begged or stolen from Ma's pocketbook for some pleasures. An ice-cream cone, soda pop, a movie down at The Dump. That's what we called the local movie theater. It was an empty store that a farseeing businessman had converted into a movie house. The first one had opened in Pittsburgh only ten years before I was born; by the time I was ready for this new form of amusement, thousands of them had sprung up in working-class and immigrant neighborhoods throughout the country. "Nice" people didn't go to the flickers until lavish movie palaces like the Poli, the Grand, and the Strand were opened in midtown. At The Dump, it was mostly kids who went, and Saturday was the day for me.

I was mesmerized by the action on the screen. It didn't matter what the story was, so long as something on that screen moved. A train rushing down the tracks to leap into my lap. A horse galloping right up and over my head. A pistol firing inches from my face. The villain attempting to plunge his knife into the heart of the frail heroine, but stopped just in the nick of time. The programs were short, and different each Saturday, for by now the moviemakers were grinding out thousands of one-reel films. Every week there was a new episode in serials that always halted at a moment of terrible danger to Pearl White or Ruth Roland so we would be sure to return next week to find out what happened next.

Like the Horatio Alger stories, many of these films gave me glimpses of life in the big city, as well as life out on the Western plains. The cowboy films were my favorites—there was an endless supply of them, starring such noble heroes as William S. Hart and Tom Mix. The stories they played in were basically as alike as were the Alger tales. But who cared. The seats and the floor were grimy and sticky with candy wrappers, well-chewed gum, lollipop fragments, and spilled sodas. The air reeked of stale food and sweat. When the lights went down to signal the start of the program we yelled, screamed, laughed, bounced madly up and down in our seats.

Silent films, they were, but if they had had sound, no one could have heard it in that bedlam. We chattered, jeered, and hissed through every foot of film. When there was kissing up there, usually by "sissiety" people in gowns and tuxedoes, we made loud smacking noises or issued long groans. We often brought something from home to nibble on, for we might stay in our seats to see the show a second or even a third time, and we got hungry. When the action became too frantic, scraps of food shot through the air toward the screen. I didn't go every week. But some kids went not only weekly but even daily, rushing down to The Dump after school.

There was live theater, too, in Worcester. Touring companies brought in the melodramas recently become popular on Broadway, but it was too expensive for us. What I did see on stage once in a while were vaudeville shows. Way up in the gallery of the Poli on Elm Street, for a dime, I watched the acts come on: magicians, tumblers, comedians, singers, dancers, animals, pianists, violinists. So far above the stage were we that the performers shrank to doll-size. But we were removed, too, from the shushing of the better-paying audience below; and surrounded by friends, we could respond almost as freely as at The Dump, roaring at the jokes, whistling in amazement at the magic, singing along with the vocalists, booing at the boring acts.

The candy store, just around the corner from us on Dorchester Street, was presided over by Hy Ruch, who always wore a white canvas apron. He made you understand quickly that, if you didn't have money, you stayed outside. But just one penny made you welcome to spend as much time as you liked, picking out treats from the trays of vivid penny-candies arrayed beneath the glass-covered counter. You pointed out your choices—one of these, two of them, and how about that one over there? And that other one just above it? Then on to the little metal-and-glass slot machine, sliding in a penny and getting in return a tiny scrap of gum or a few jelly beans. Hy let you linger inside while you rolled those morsels in your mouth. Then you wandered over to the reading racks, ignoring the newspapers, thumbing through the piles of Algers and Merriwells and Nick Carters, sneaking a perverse look at the *Police Gazette*, with its full-page displays of women overflowing their bathing suits as they winked lecherously at you.

Hy didn't care how little you were, so long as you had that penny or nickel or dime. And once inside that small shop—not much more than a wooden hut, it stood alone on the corner— you were king among consumers. Like rich women in the downtown department stores, you could carefully examine the offerings, deliberate over your choices, and feel like a grown-up when you completed a transaction. It took so little to make you feel so privileged.

At times I supplied free messenger service for Hy. He had a pay telephone in the store. Lots of people couldn't afford their own phone. (We had to have one, for my father's business. I still remember our number: Park 311OR.) So Hy's phone became the neighborhood's communications center. If I were in the store, and Mrs. Kaplowitz phoned to say she wanted to talk to Mrs. Aronowitz, Hy would send me flying over to Mrs. A.'s with the message. If Mrs. A. felt good, she'd give me a nickel. Every kid who dropped in performed that service when needed.

No one made long-distance calls casually in those days. They were only for emergencies or special occasions. Well in advance, my mother would inform my grandparents by letter to expect a call on Sunday night at 7. On the appointed hour, Ma would call the operator to place the call, and ask her to cut in with a warning when the minimum time, three minutes, was up. When Grandma in New York answered the phone, my mother would say excitedly, "What's the weather there?" Grandma would turn in equal excitement to her family and call out, "Mary wants to

know what the weather is!" Then she'd say, "It's raining here!"
And Ma would turn to us and call, "Grandma says it's raining
in New York!" And she would inform Grandma, "It's raining
by us here, too!" And Grandma would yell to the family at her
end, "It's raining with them, too!" By the time these prelimi-
naries were over, so were the three minutes. Nothing of sub-
stance was said by anyone. Over the operator's solemn insistence
that the time was up, Ma and Grandma would promise each
other to write again to say when they'd make the next call.

More venturesome than the frequent forays into Hy's candy
store was a journey to Water Street. It was the main shopping
center for the Jewish community. Once an Irish neighborhood,
it had turned largely Jewish by my time. Only a few blocks long,
it was a jumble of brick buildings with tenements above and
stores below—small stores, hot in summer and cold in winter.
I walked the mile or so to Water Street on an occasional Sunday
morning, bearing my mother's shopping list. You could buy
some of these things closer to home but, for quality, everyone
considered the Water Street stores the best: Whitman's cream-
ery, Weintraub's delicatessen, Arkus's pharmacy. And Apelbaum's tiny shop was the only place in town to buy the Yiddish
newspapers. The *Forward*, or *Forvitz* as they called it, was the
socialist paper and the most popular and influential. Then there
was the *Tag*, the *Journal*, the *Tageblatt*, and even the *Freiheit*,
a Communist paper. My father asked for the *Tag* now and then.
Like most of the Jewish stores, Apelbaum's was open every day
in the year except for Rosh Hashanah and Yom Kippur. And
from early in the morning until the last customer had left at
night. Along one wall were cubbyholes with names above them,
for the regulars who wanted the same paper every day. Mr.
Apelbaum trudged over to Union Station each morning to pick
up the papers from the New York train, and carried them to

his store by wagon or sled. He handled special orders, too: getting any Jewish book you wanted from New York, or sheet music, or tickets to the Jewish shows that came to town.

Arkus's filled not only prescriptions but also your appetite for delicious sodas and sundaes. His soda fountain ranged along the right side of the store, and on the left were a couple of round glass-topped tables with those curlicued metal chairs that always seemed to go with eating ice cream topped with his splendid homemade chocolate syrup.

By now the variety of foods you could get in America—when you could afford it—was taken for granted by my mother and father. But to Ben and Mary, the abundance they discovered when they arrived as immigrants was astounding. For example, bananas, oranges, and grapefruit, once luxuries, had only recently become plentiful as refrigerated boats and boxcars brought them north. But it took some time before they became cheap enough to reach the working-class table. It was amazing—not only the number of foods for sale and the different forms they came in. Vegetables, fruits, meats, and soups were sold in cans as well as fresh. The tinned products of Campbell, Libby, and Heinz became part of the daily diet that had only yesterday been rigidly limited. Now they could put peas on the table, in winter!

What had been sweet delights only for the aristocracy back in Bukovina or Galicia were now common pleasures. I mean the taste of sugar, chocolate, candy, ice cream, soft drinks. All these joys Arkus and the corner candy store dispensed. We didn't buy the commercial Coke or Moxie or Dr. Pepper. Instead, we gulped glasses of homemade root beer. Ma prepared huge pots of it regularly in the summer, using Hire's extract as the starter. When a batch was ready, I poured it through a funnel into our glass bottles, snapped the metal-and-rubber cap shut, and toted the wooden cases of root beer out to our back porch and into the woodshed for storage, leaving several bottles to chill in the icebox.

The best sweets were not store-bought but homemade. My mother was a great cook and baker. Regularly on Friday, she baked honey buns, coffee cake, schnecken, apple or cherry or blueberry pies. She made fine challah, corn, and rye bread. I remember her standing next to the big black wood-burning stove in our kitchen, slicing the warm bread as she held it against her breast.

Yes, we ate well. Breakfast was usually stewed prunes with a dash of milk, a hot cereal of oatmeal, Wheatena, farina or Cream of Wheat, or sometimes a cold one—shredded wheat taken out of that box with the picture of Niagara Falls on it. The noon meal during the school term was a hurry-up grab of leftovers during the short recess period. For supper, there might be a pot roast with mashed potatoes and gravy, chicken on Friday, perhaps a rib steak on Sunday.

Helping Ma with the root beer was but one of the chores she demanded of each of her sons in turn, as we grew old enough to handle them. She had no notion that some kinds of work were for women only, and that men should not be expected to do them. I made my bed, dusted the furniture, and dry-mopped the floors every single day. She was maniacal in her insistence on cleanliness, neatness, order, regularity. When she had finished scrubbing the week's laundry by hand on the washboard, my job was to wring out the batch, take it to the back porch, and hang it with wooden clothespins on the reel of rope stretched across the open space. In winter, the clothes often froze stiff as corrugated iron, the long johns looking like grotesque human figures. When the wash was dry, my next job was to iron—sheets, pillowcases, towels, and to do the more careful pressing of shirts and pants without scorching them with the heavy metal iron. I was in big trouble if I did.

Ma found it hard to forgive human error. Perfection was her natural standard. It even extended to sleep. I remember I slept on my back when young, and never seemed to move in the night, so that when I woke in the morning the sheet was smooth and flat, without a wrinkle. Maybe I was trying to show Ma I didn't mess things up even while asleep. As for how long you slept, she had fixed ideas there, too. To stay abed more than eight hours was a gross offense. "Lazy good-for-nothing!" she'd exclaim, usually routing me out of bed only minutes past the allotted time. This, even when I tried to sneak in an extra hour or two when school was out and an idle day stretched ahead. Idle? When was there a time when something didn't have to be done? I didn't have to ask. She told me, firmly and loudly.

Her craze for neatness affected how we dressed, of course. Ma had her eye peeled for the latest styles. She stayed abreast of them by studying the clothing ads in the newspapers, and by window-shopping in the big department stores downtown. Somehow she saw to it that I was dressed well and kept my clothes clean and neat. She herself was as good a seamstress and tailor as she was a cook and baker. She would find the right patterns and sew or knit well-chosen materials to make us shirts and sweaters and mackinaws. I still remember my elation when I strutted out with my brand-new checkered mackinaw she had made of a bold black-and-red heavy flannel. Naturally, with our family income, hand-me-downs were taken for granted. Allan wore the new stuff first, then me, then Marshall.

Now and then, we got new suits and shoes from the shops downtown. Ware Pratt was a men's and boy's store on the ground floor of the Slater Building on Main Street. Ten stories high, it was the tallest building in town, and my father rented a closet in it where he stored his window-cleaning equipment and work clothes. An expedition with Ma to Ware Pratt made me edgy. Would she buy something I liked? Or make me take what she liked? Usually I came away pleased. A three-piece suit back then cost $10. Not a small sum when you consider the weekly wage for workers was only $15.

Ware Pratt tried to make you their customer for life by entering your name on a birthday register. Every year, they notified you to come down and pick up your free birthday cake with your name etched in icing. The first time my brother Marshall went to get his, he came home so excited that he tripped and fell running up our stairs, and crushed his cake.

I think we were the best-dressed boys in the neighborhood, much to Allan's disgust. Fearlessly, he would dirty or rip new clothing to show the guys he was no sissified dandy. It deepened Ma and Pa's despair of his ever growing up to be anything but a bum. I quaked at the storms of rage his behavior evoked. I never imitated it, though I wished sometimes that I had the courage for open defiance. My rebellion was sneaky, like when I swiped small change out of a purse or a drawer. Or brought in Stella secretly. Or waited till Ma and Pa were asleep and then read my book by flashlight under the blanket.

Fifteen Cents an Hour

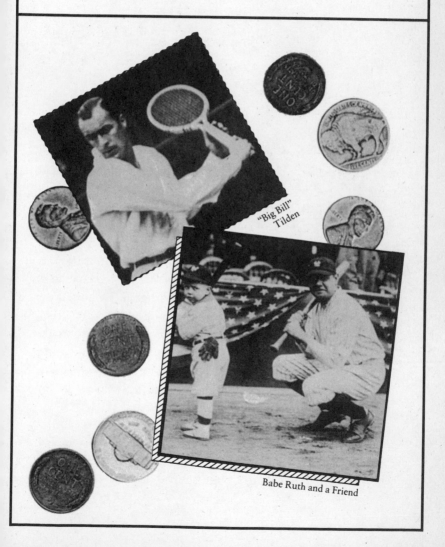

"Big Bill" Tilden

Babe Ruth and a Friend

I was in junior high when I began to work. We Meltzer sons were expected to pitch in and help the family. I had a newspaper route for a while, delivering the afternoon *Post* in our neighborhood. A little later, I moved up the scale. Sam Reed, who lived on the first floor of our three-decker, was the office manager at a wholesale grocery firm on Grafton Street. He arranged for me to work there after school, and Saturday mornings. It was a huge, dimly lit cavern, that building, with enormous stacks of crates and cartons climbing into the heights. I wheeled the heavy loads of packaged and canned goods on a hand truck from one spot to another or to the loading docks where trucks carried them off to grocery stores. It was hard and dull work, but I hoped that doing a man's job would build up real muscle. Pay? 15 cents an hour. I kept 50 cents each week out of my pay envelope and handed the couple of dollars left to Ma.

A much better job came my way the next summer. I worked for a milk company, on a neighborhood route. Barney Quigley, the driver, picked me up at 2 A.M. I got up in the dark, dressed without putting on the light, then slipped down the two flights of stairs to the backyard and out to the street, where Barney was always waiting, the tip of his cigarette glowing in the dark behind the windshield. I hopped in beside him and we'd talk till we reached the beginning of our route. Then I'd go around the back and balance on the tailboard, leaning into the truck, grab a metal rack, fill it with bottles, and jump down, taking the customers on my side of the street while he'd take the other side. He was a little slower, for he was a lot older, of course, and he limped.

One bottle on the first floor for the widow Polasewicz, up the stairs and five bottles for the big Murphy family, up another flight for two milks and the cream Mrs. Gould had to have. I learned fast what every customer took. Then I'd go clattering down the steps, picking up the empties along the way. Back to the truck, stow the empties to one side, load another rack for the next three-decker.

Here and there, we'd stop at grocery stores to drop off cases of milk in their doorways. Best part of the night was when we'd both feel hungry (around four it usually was), and we'd swipe a fresh-baked loaf from the baskets the bakery truck would leave at the grocers, and tear off big mouthfuls, washing down the delicious crusts of warm bread with swigs of cold milk.

It would be almost daylight by the time our truck would pull up again in front of my house. Barney would reach into his pocket, dig out a dollar, and hand it to me. "So long!" Then the climb upstairs, an orange out of the icebox, deep bites into the juicy flesh, a lingering look at the early morning sun gliding from window to window, and bed.

In the beginning, I ached all over so badly I might have quit if the family didn't need the money. I never knew you could feel so tired, arms and legs turned to lead, back sore, fingers stiff. The first few times I flopped into bed after dawn, I slept all through the day. But gradually my muscles got tougher and I could swing those bottles through the night, sleep six hours, and be ready for anything.

I loved working with Barney that summer. He didn't treat me like a kid. Once, when Barney stumbled and fell getting down from the truck, I asked him was he sick. "No," he said, "it's that damned knee," patting it. He'd been a Marine in the war in France, and a shell fragment had hit him. They put a plate in his knee, but he never walked right again. He was the first veteran I'd met, and I wanted to know what the war was like. "Like nothing you'll ever want to see," he said. "Don't be no hero. I was married, but I went anyway. 'The Yanks Are Coming' and I wanted to be one of 'em." Then he laughed. "But what you got to worry about? My war's hardly over. Won't be another that soon, will there?"

I found out that the reason I, and not his son, was his helper, was that they didn't get along very well. The boy did badly at school, hated it, and always had the truant officer after him. He was painting houses that summer. Every boy I knew was working, if he could find a job. Nothing special about it. It wasn't a choice for you if your parents were working-class. What property did they own? What education did they have? What money in the bank? When the work they did paid so little, it was taken for granted that their children would help. Millions of families, like mine, earned less than $1,000 a year—$20 a week. So we hustled. Unlike the boy heroes of the Alger stories, I didn't expect to get rich. But neither did I expect to work the way my father did.

I never saw him go off to work until that summer I was delivering milk. Then I found he got up at the same time I did, at 2 A.M. It was fun for me, but for him? He did it every day, every week, all the year round. He walked downtown through the dead streets because no streetcars ran at that hour. His first round of work was to clean the big plate-glass windows of the four Waldorf cafeterias scattered through the business district. The job had to be finished by 6 A.M., when the breakfast crowds came flooding in. That done, he moved on to factories, stores, and offices to clean their windows. After midday, he did the windows of private homes on the west side, where the well-to-do lived. He'd return home sometimes by 2 P.M. and often as late as 4. His was a 12- to 14-hour day. It brought us a modest living.

Late one afternoon in midwinter, I came out of the main library, where I had borrowed a book I needed. That winter had dragged on without any of the thaws that sometimes eased the harsh New England weather. One snow on top of another, huge drifts, and when it seemed the sun must break through, a fresh fall to renew the white nightmare. I boarded a streetcar that was worming its way slowly through the icy snow. I was deep in my book when I heard a harsh cough, then another and another, coming from a passenger several seats down from me. I glanced up from the page, and saw that it was my father, racked by his chain-smoker's cough. He was almost asleep, his head nodding, his legs slumped into the aisle, his shoulders shaking now and then as the cough persisted.

I studied him as though he were a stranger. The long years of work in all weathers had etched his skin like acid. His leathery face had two deep crevices running from the corners of his mouth upward. His hands were almost black, his fingers and palms crisscrossed with cuts and cracks made by water, wind, ice, snow, and freezing cold. Never lifting his eyes, he didn't notice me. When our stop came at the corner of Providence and Dorchester, he got up to leave, going past me but still not seeing me. I rose after him, walking behind him to the exit, suddenly aware how bent his back had become, his spine curved by the endless hours of labor in that position. As I got down from the trolley, I called out, "Pa!" He turned, waited for me to catch up. Then reached out and stroked my cheek, a rare gesture for him. His fingers felt like sandpaper on my face.

Life, of course, was not just school and work. Pleasure was possible at any season of the year. In the long Massachusetts winters, I took out my Flexible Flyer sled to coast down Union Hill, belly-whopping alone or two sitting up. To protect us, the street was closed to traffic for a couple of hours after school. But once in a while, there was delicious danger. I remember a truck suddenly skidding out of a side street and my sled zipping under it and on down the hill to the end, where I offered myself to the other kids as a hero.

I learned to skate on the pond at Vernon Hill Park. The skates were a blade welded to a flat sheet of steel cut roughly to the shape of the foot. On both sides of the sole and heel were clamps you turned with a screw, fastening the skate to your shoe. The whole thing was held tight with a strap that crossed from one side of the heel and over the foot to the other side. Little kids had double-runner blades to assure their balance. As I grew older, shoe skates came into fashion. That is, skate and shoe were made as one. Neat! First I had a pair of hockey skates— short blades for quick starts and turns—and then advanced to hand-me-down racing skates. These had very long slim blades that guaranteed I'd break speed records. Night-skating was the best. The stars overhead, dim forms winding in and out over the moonlit ice, a fire on shore, swooping flights or graceful figures intended to enthrall the girls.

I swam in the same pond in the summer, and, when old enough, hitchhiked to Lake Quinsigamond. It was at the lake that I learned to swim, when very young. I was invited by the

Masons, neighbors in my first home on Chapin Street, to come spend a week or two at their summer cottage on the lake. The cottages, small and simple, were lined along the shore, with a small patch of grass between them. My bed was always damp and moldy. But just beyond the front door was the Masons' own wharf jutting into the water. I didn't know how to swim the first time I visited, but within a few days, Clare Mason and her boyfriend Tom overcame my fears. Hesitantly, I waded out to where the water was just over my head, and suddenly I was swimming. I don't know how; it just happened. I couldn't swim, and then I could.

For one or two summers when I was very small, my father managed to send the family to Revere Beach, outside Boston, for a couple of weeks. He didn't take time for a vacation, and showed up just for the weekend. We took the train from Worcester to Boston, then shifted to a narrow-gauge railway for the short run to the beach. My mother rented a room in a boardinghouse a few blocks from the ocean. Every morning, I toted pail and shovel down to the shore to dig in the sand, and Allan and I took turns burying each other up to the neck. My mother swapped news and gossip with the other mothers as the children soaked up the sun. Not yet a swimmer, I just dashed in and out of the surf, yelling and splashing water on the other kids. Sometimes music blared over the beach from the bandstand where the musicians sweated under a metal roof.

When Pa came down for the weekend, he took us all out for a big treat. We ate at Gordon's, the first time I ever had a meal in a restaurant. Soup, chopped liver on rye, pie, ice cream, soda—nothing I had not had before. But to dine in a great big room with hundreds of other people at tables around us, talking and laughing while we all ate so much we could barely make it to the beach afterwards? That was special! The one other event of that time I remember was the day newsboys zigzagged across the sand yelling, "EXTRA! EXTRA! CARUSO DEAD." "Who's Caruso?" I asked Ma. "A great singer," she said. Later I found the tenor had died in 1921, so I was six then, Allan was nine, and Marshall was one.

The summer that stands out best in my mind came when I was nine. I was invited to spend a few weeks on a farm in the Catskills, near Kingston. It was run by my father's sister, Aunt Vitya, and her husband, Uncle Louis Ludwig. Although Worcester was the center of a rural county, I had never been on a farm. I went by train to Kingston and was picked up by Uncle Louis in his car. For company, there were my three cousins, Jack, Marty and Milly. They all had chores to do and I followed them around each day, seeing how cows and chickens and horses were cared for, and how crops were tended. That summer gave me my first view of the sex act, at least as performed by animals. My cousins paid no attention to it, and laughed at how I couldn't stop staring.

The talk at table was dull for me—all about farm prices and equipment and crop yields. Until a sensational criminal trial burst into the headlines and had the whole country discussing it. Two rich boys in Chicago, Nathan Leopold and Richard Loeb, were on trial for the kidnapping and murder of another boy, Robert Franks. It was the first I heard of the famous trial lawyer Clarence Darrow. He opposed capital punishment and was the first to put up a defense based on psychiatric evidence, which resulted in Leopold and Loeb getting life sentences. I remember Marty asking how come this lawyer who always defended the underdog was taking the case of these rich kids? Uncle Louis said that every accused person has the right to the best defense he can get. Later, in high school, I read Darrow's book *The Story of My Life*. What courage he had to take up unpopular causes! He often defended the underdog—labor organizers, socialists, minorities.

Once, years before this, I made my first trip to New York. It was the Passover and Easter season, when school was out, and my mother wanted us to celebrate the Seder with my grandparents in New York. Pa, of course, did not go; he stayed behind, working. We took the train, lugging a big suitcase and a brown bag with sandwiches Ma had packed. When the candy peddler paraded the aisle calling out, "Candy! Soda! Ice Cream!" Ma gave in to our begging and bought whatever we asked for.

We had boarded the train at 1 P.M., eager to see the countryside and the towns we'd pass through. But the windows were so grimy, and the train rushed by so fast, we saw little. At New Haven the steam locomotive was taken off and an electric one put on. We rolled into Grand Central at 6 P.M. Ma never thought to let us see the center of the city. She hustled us into the subway bound for the Bronx and we raced underground for a long time till we reached the station near Samuel and Rose Richter's tenement, on Dawson Street.

We stayed several days, slept on folding cots, ate huge meals, and I fell asleep during the Seder which Grandpa drew out to the last syllable of the Haggadah. I was bewildered by a host of aunts and uncles and their friends and the constant coming and going. The peak of that visit came when Uncle Harry took me to Yankee Stadium so I could see a major-league ball game. We sat just behind the Yankee dugout. I was awed by the sight of Babe Ruth in action, though he hit no homer that afternoon. But I was even more impressed when my uncle pointed out Walter Winchell, the gossip columnist everyone listened to on the radio Sunday nights or read in the papers. I couldn't wait to get back home to tell the gang.

I was 12 when I began to play tennis. I don't know how it

happened, for I was the only boy in our neighborhood who tried the game. The others considered it sissy stuff. Baseball, football, basketball, boxing—they knew everything about those sports and could spout the statistics by the hour, while I knew little and cared little. But somehow the occasional pictures in the newspapers of the players in the major tennis tournaments drew my eye. The men all looked tall, blond, handsome, debonair in their white flannels. I'd picture myself dashing about a tennis court looking just as graceful and just as elegant.

I knew there were a few public courts at Vernon Hill Park, where I'd gone swimming many times. I began to hang around those courts, watching the boys and girls play the game. Gradually I got to know some of them, and one boy, who had two rackets, loaned me one so I could try it. Of course I was awful. But I kept at it, and eventually learned to play a decent game. There was no pro at the public courts. You learned by watching better players and trying to follow what they did. Without lessons, it was all too easy to pick up bad habits and groove them so deeply it became hard to rid yourself of them. But still, I was good enough to find plenty of partners for singles or doubles. Two boys especially stood out: one was Jordan Cotton, short and plump, not my image of a star, but a beautiful stylist and a pleasure to watch. The other was Dave Porter, tall and rangy, with powerful strokes. Later he captained my high school's tennis team. I came to enjoy the game far more than swimming, and on Sunday mornings I'd hitch to a public park on Lake Quinsigamond where there were asphalt courts rarely in use. If I got there early enough, I could play for two, three, and even four hours.

I began following tennis on the sports pages. I had as much to say about "Big Bill" Tilden as the other kids did about Babe Ruth or Jack Dempsey. Only they didn't want to hear it. Tennis became so consuming a passion that, with a friend, I hitched a ride to Boston one summer day in order to see the national doubles championship played at the Longwood Club. We circled the club till we found an old elm standing tall just outside the wall, and invisible from the gate. We shinned up the trunk, crawled out on a thick branch, and dropped inside. We stayed all day, wildly excited to see the world's best players close up. Tennis fans in those days were mostly upper-class; we must have looked strange and shabby to the elite. But no one paid attention to us. I felt by the end of the afternoon that surely I'd play ten times better after seeing how the champions did it. Of course I was wrong.

Becoming Somebody

"Lucky Lindy,"
1927

Culver Pictures

1924: Ku Klux Klan,
"Can he shake it off?"

My years at junior high reached a grand climax when I was elected president of the graduating class. I was 14, and at last I had become a "somebody." Not that I worked for it. I didn't campaign for the office; it simply happened as the outcome of student balloting. But it pleased me enormously, for I had secretly been trying to become a somebody. One means was by changing my handwriting. Trained by strict teachers to write with the letters slanting to the right, I think when I was about 13 I decided to write with the opposite slant—to the left, or backwards. It was hard to do consistently after years of the other style, but I kept at it. I must have been very eager to appear different. I'd look at my handwriting and say, Now there's something special about me! I had made myself distinctive, and in a visible way. At least to the teachers who had to go over my homework.

Another path to being a somebody was to modify my name. *Meltzer*. That wasn't too bad, though people have a hard time getting it right. When they hear me say it they repeat it inaccurately: *Neltzner,* or *Melter,* or *Melzer,* so early on, I took to spelling it out as soon as I said it, and I still do that. Does my name mean anything? *Goldsmith* or *Taylor* or *Carpenter*: I knew what such names meant. I used to think of my name as simply a Jewish one, because the only other Meltzers I knew were Jewish. Until, much later, I read that one of Hitler's generals was a Meltzer. I doubted *he* was Jewish. I looked into it, and found there was a small town in Germany called Meltz; the "er" ending can simply mean someone from that place. In Polish, it can mean a brewer. In Hebrew, the word *meltzer* means "waiter." (See the Bible, Daniel 1:16.)

I never warmed to *Milton,* but neither would I discard it. I couldn't figure out how Ma and Pa had come up with that name. I'm sure they didn't know (I learned it much later) that it comes from old English, and means "town near the mill." I doubted they had ever read, or heard of, the poet John Milton. As a surname, it was fine. But as a first name? I used to try variants of its sound: *Hilton, Wilton, Stilton,* hoping it would make me feel better. It didn't. I felt bad about it until a movie star appeared on the silent screen with the name of Milton Sills. He was big, powerful, a handsome leading man. If Milton was good enough for *him*, it was good enough for me.

What I did do about my name was to invent a middle one. Almost everybody I knew had three names. Why only two for me? Odd that this bothered me, since I wanted to be different, and two names caused teachers taking the roll for the first time to say, "No middle name?" At least that singled me out! But in my last year in junior high, I began putting down my name as Milton Morey Meltzer. More style, that *Morey*, more class, more dignity. I never asked anyone to call me that, just wrote it wherever school papers or records required my name. How I came up with Morey, I'm not sure. I think I wanted the alliterative effect of three M's and the drumbeat of the repeated two syllables.

Perhaps I was thinking of the Frank Merriwell stories in which the Yale students' favorite hangout was a place called Morey's. At any rate, that name appears on my records for the three years I would spend at Classical High School. (I dropped it when I left for college.)

It was January 1930 when I finished junior high. Only some four weeks before, in October 1929, an earthquake shook the foundations of American life. I was completely unaware of it. There had been an unexpected and severe break in stock-market prices. The market plunged sickeningly. Panic seized Wall Street. Every day, the losses were worse and worse. Overnight, the life savings of many went down the drain. The disaster on Wall Street signaled the onset of the Great Depression. It was a signal I didn't catch. Nothing was said about it at our table, or in the neighborhood. Families like ours, the vast majority of Americans, did not feel the shock wave at once. We didn't "go broke" in the Depression. Ma and Pa had *started* broke in the America they had adopted. They owned no stocks and didn't even know what they were. All we owned were our clothes and our furniture. Soon, however, we found out that you didn't have to own stock to feel the impact of the crash.

The shock spread rapidly from Wall Street to the poorest unskilled worker. Still, it wasn't the rich who became poor. The "big money," the owners of the great American fortunes, were able to hang onto their wealth. A big cut below them were the middle class, people like those who lived on Worcester's west side, the prosperous. If a family earned $6,000 a year in the Twenties, it put them in that class. It sounds like very little today, but in the Twenties we didn't know anyone who earned that kind of money. Yes, Pa worked for them, cleaning the windows of their homes and stores and offices, but they weren't friends of the family.

A bracket below these people were those earning less than $3,000 a year. That took in four out of five American families. And about a third of this group had incomes under $1,000 a year. Miners, lumbermen, people doing hard, dirty, dangerous work, earned only some $10 a week.

My family was sandwiched somewhere in those lower layers. Ma and Pa had no bank account. What could they save? The only way they could add to the bare necessities of life was by buying on credit—"a dollar a day and a dollar forever." Not for Ma and Pa. Pay-as-you-go was their creed. If you can't afford it, don't get it. So we had a tub and a scrubbing board and Ma's muscle, not a washing machine. An icebox, not a refrigerator. A mop and a carpet-sweeper, not a vacuum cleaner. And never an automobile. The only exception to the rule I can remember was the weekly visit of an insurance agent to our home. He came to collect from Ma the 10 cents a week she paid for a $500 life insurance policy. She had to make sure that if someone died, there was money to bury him.

So the Roaring Twenties—that catchphrase glued to the decade of my childhood—was no boom time for us or for a vast number of other Americans. If the Twenties were so prosperous, where did the money go? The cream was skimmed off the top. The richest Americans—5 percent at the top—controlled about one-third of all personal income. They invested their money at high interest rates and paid almost no income tax. I remember reading in Walter Winchell's gossip column that it was the habit of a certain celebrity to tip his waiter at the Plaza Hotel a $20 bill. Pa had to clean 133 windows (at 15 cents apiece) to earn that much money.

But middle-class people believed in the American dream of

unlimited plenty. And I think even families like ours, remote from the rich, shared in the mood. Every city had its speakeasies, the illegal bars where you could get liquor during the Prohibition years. The flappers—girls wearing bobbed hair and short skirts—could be seen on any Main Street. And the new music! Jazz and the blues blaring out of millions of radios and record players. Even our family had a radio. At first it was a tiny crystal set. I clamped on the earphones and then poked the wire tickler into various spots on the small crystal till I picked up the local radio station, WTAG, and heard voices or music. Later we got a Silver Marshall radio, with a glossy walnut-finish cabinet that became the centerpiece of our parlor. I often stayed up late Saturday nights to catch the rhythmic jolts of the great jazz bands on remote pickups from ballrooms or hotels around the country: McKinney's Cotton Pickers, Duke Ellington, Earl Hines, Jimmy Lunceford, Fletcher Henderson.

By the end of the Twenties I had lived through the terms of four Presidents. I was born when Woodrow Wilson was in office, and was quite unaware of his crusade "to make the world safe for democracy." Then the good-time years of Warren Harding, the tall handsome Ohioan who, like President Reagan, seemed cast for the role, and who let private oil barons exploit public lands. After a Senate investigation, one of his Cabinet members went to jail, while the President's other cronies either committed suicide or fled the country.

Harding died rather mysteriously in office when I was eight. And Calvin Coolidge, a trim, purse-mouthed Yankee from my home state, Massachusetts, stepped up from the Vice-presidency. "The business of America is business," he announced, anticipating Ronald Reagan by some sixty years. By doing little and saying less, he won a reputation for wisdom. Young as I was, I remember the many jokes circulating about him:

"Did you hear? President Coolidge is dead!"
"How can they tell?"

The stock market was soaring, and prosperity (for the lucky ones) was in full flood in 1928 when Coolidge chose not to run again. A vicious note struck in that presidential campaign reached down into our neighborhood and made me conscious of politics for the first time. Herbert Hoover, an engineer of considerable achievement, was nominated by the Republicans. His opponent was Al Smith, the liberal Governor of New York. As an Irish Catholic, Smith was the victim of a carefully orchestrated "whispering" campaign that played on religious prejudice. The Republicans, with the help of the Ku Klux Klan, spread it about that if Al Smith entered the White House, the Pope would come to Washington to run the country. I remember hearing echoes of that charge on the street. Some of the Irish-Catholic kids—the Murphys, Grogans, Falveys—were taunted with it, and we Jews felt uneasy about the appeal to a nasty prejudice. At that very moment, Hitler and the Nazis were climbing to power in Germany on the same kind of prejudice. Hoover won, with 58 percent of the popular vote. (Not until 1960, 32 years later, would a Catholic, John F. Kennedy, barely make it to the Presidency.)

As for myself, I had mixed feelings about Catholics. I played with the Murphy boys; they lived on Vale Street, too. And while in a game, never thought about them as anything but kids like me. Yet when I went into their home, the colored pictures on their walls made me shudder. Jesus on the cross, bleeding, agonized. Saints pierced by swords or arrows, their eyes lifted piteously to heaven. The Virgin Mary, mourning. Dick and Tom didn't seem even to notice them, but I couldn't take my eyes off the pictures. Didn't Catholics enjoy themselves? Sure, on the playground or at Christmas. But why such gloom on the wall? What does it all mean, I wanted to know. I couldn't ask, either the boys or anyone else. When I passed a Catholic church I'd cross the street to the other side, I don't know why. Once, when walking with another Jewish boy, we saw a nun in black habit coming toward us. Bernie turned his head and spit deliberately into the gutter. "What did you do that for?" I asked. "You have to," he said. "It's bad luck if you don't."

Yet it was easy to fall in love with Alice Falvey when I was in junior high. She was the pretty daughter of an Irish cop in our neighborhood. All we did was to go for a walk now and then. But one day, when I was in the grocery store to help Ma carry home the bundles, a woman sidled up to her and said, "So your boy is going with a *shiksa*, that Falvey girl, huh?" "What!" said Ma, and turning instantly, smacked me hard across the face. I ran out of the store, humiliated and furious.

In school, nothing was said about political and social problems, or about prejudice and racism. We had classes in civics and current events, but the first only talked of the formal structure of government, never the way it really worked, and the other simply checked to see if we read the headlines, without digging beneath for their meaning.

Anyway, the general run of news didn't grab my attention. Though I wasn't a baseball fan, the fact that Babe Ruth was breaking all records with his home runs was somehow thrilling. And when Gene Tunney won the heavyweight championship from Jack Dempsey before a huge crowd that paid millions to see the fight, that was thrilling, too. But the climax in pride and excitement came in May 1927 when Charles Lindbergh, "Lucky Lindy," landed in Paris to complete the first nonstop solo flight across the Atlantic. I came running out with the other kids to scream, "He made it! He made it!" It was only a few years before that historic flight that we used to pause at whatever game we were playing to point up in the sky and chant, "Air-o-plane! Air-o-plane!" whenever one of those strange, rare birds flew overhead.

Living in Two Worlds

Anna Shaughnessy

"The Club"
with me,
front and center

When the 1930s began, I entered Classical High. As the child of a family to whom everything American was new, the ancient history of this school impressed me. Classical High was nearly 100 years old. Earlier, when it was known as the Latin Grammar School, John Adams, fresh out of Harvard, had taught there. I wanted badly to go there. There were a few other high schools in Worcester, but this was rated the best. That is, if you wished to go to college. It offered a traditional classical education. The world of commerce and industry was ignored. If you expected to go into office work or the trades, you were steered elsewhere.

No relative of mine, either in the old country or in America, had gone to college. Yet I knew that somehow I would go, even though there was no money for it. Scholarships were rare and hard to win; few cities had public colleges where tuition was free. Only a tiny percentage of high school students went on to college. Few of these were working-class.

Then what made me think college was for me? Perhaps it was because I was born curious. I loved to read, to explore new ideas, to meet new people and go to new places, whether in books or in real life. The more I learned, the more there was to be learned. It was boundless, this world of knowledge and experience. I thought of teachers as bottomless wells of information. How lucky they were to be surrounded by books, nourished by books. Early on I began to think I'd like to be a teacher. And to be able to do that, wouldn't I have to go to college?

It was around this time that I began to experience a dream of delight, over and over again. In my dream I floated up off my bed and then flew around the room like a small bird, soaring, swooping, marveling at how easy it was and how graceful and free. I felt an exaltation such as I rarely experienced in waking hours. The dream recurred again and again, for years.

Perhaps the dream expressed a confidence in the future, an optimism about myself and where I was going. Certain I would be a teacher, I knew that Classical High and then college were meant for me.

There was another side to my ambition, however. It had to do with being Jewish. I think I've already said that my family had pushed aside the synagogue. That didn't mean denying their Jewishness. My mother and father, as I see them now, were conscious of living in two worlds, wanting to forget the painful part of their past, and eager to embrace their future. A reason why they did not pass on to me their memories of the old world? Whatever America thought foreign I think they wanted to discard. So they moved in a limited way to adopt the new kind of life. They took on its customs, its manners, its language as best they could. Yiddish was rarely spoken in our home, and usually only when Pa and Ma wanted to conceal something from us. Still, the rhythm of their speech, the style of their gestures, the values of the culture they brought with them, made their imprint on me.

While I felt secure within the family, I yearned to be accepted outside. I looked forward eagerly to Classical High because there I would meet far more "Americans." Not "Italian-Americans," not "Jewish-Americans," just plain *Americans*. The unhyphenated people. The native-born for generations, the rooted, the settled, the self-confident. It wasn't that I believed my own parents were inferior because they were foreign. It was rather that I wanted to make myself into a "real American." Now I remember with shame that I used to feel pleased when Gentiles told me that they didn't know I was Jewish: "You don't look it!" To be more like them was an irresistible desire. America and Americans were so glorified that it was no wonder the child of immigrants wanted passionately to be exactly like those Americans.

In our neighborhood, there were few people of that kind to get to know or to imitate. Almost everyone was an immigrant or the child of immigrants. The "Yankees" lived on the other side of town, the west side. And it was in their school, Classical, that I knew I'd meet these dream people.

The Classical High building was on a quiet corner just off the center of the city. A huge, squared-off redstone tower rose five stories high into a dormered hip roof. Flanking it were two wings of three-and-a-half stories, sitting solidly on a granite base. The two entries had elaborate carvings, the windows were very tall, and the doors were all oak-paneled. It was massive, dignified, just the right look for a college-prep school.

I was dismayed at first by how different most of the students seemed from me. They had Anglo-Saxon names, they dressed casually but expensively, they spoke a precise English, they played golf, they went to country club dances. They were graceful, relaxed, sure of themselves. I felt both alien to all that and at the same time envious of it. I soon found they were no brighter, or dumber, than the rest of us. But they had "class." For a long time I was shy and anxious in their presence.

Most of the courses were required; little choice was left to me. I began with English, French, Latin, and algebra. Later, geometry, biology, physics, and history (ancient, modern European and American) were added. The men and women who taught us were quite capable. Many had gone to the best colleges, and took teaching seriously as an honorable profession. Usually they taught in the traditional manner: textbooks, lots of homework, recitations, written essays, and frequent exams. You could learn a great deal, many things, facts mostly, if you cared to.

Ideas? No, there was little said about them. Few teachers made any attempt to get us to think. What they did ask of us was to remember—facts, dates, theorems, laws of government or of physics, the succession of kings or presidents, classifications of plants and animals, rules of grammar—and only long enough to spew them back on paper at testing time. With few exceptions, they did not ask us to think critically, or give us any hint of how to do that. Such teaching kills the natural curiosity, instead of encouraging it. What too many students learned best was how to con the teacher and beat the system.

When I look back at the schools I went to, they seem like some kind of mildly authoritarian society. They meant well, but they didn't allow for democracy in the classroom. The principal ordered the teachers around and they in turn ordered us around. Our sole responsibility was to come to class, to come on time, and to do our assignments. A few students rebelled against the rigid discipline, but in a way that only did harm to themselves and brought about no change for the better.

The shining exception to these teachers was Anna Shaughnessy, a graduate of Radcliffe. She was Irish and Catholic (like so many of our teachers), young, tall, and very thin. She wore glasses, and kept her brown hair in a bun. Her brilliance, her sparkling wit, delighted us. English was her field, but her mind roamed free over all the world of knowledge. Whether it was *Hamlet* or a poem of Browning's or a novel by George Eliot, in her class it became far more than an assignment to be gotten through dutifully. She paid close attention to the text of the work, but more, she brought in the lives of the writers, the world they lived in, the influences that shaped their ideas and the language that gave form to them. You could speak up freely in her class, say whatever you felt and thought, without fear of being made to look foolish or ignorant. If she caught you faking, she could be caustic. But so long as you tried honestly to grapple with what you were reading, you were encouraged. She challenged everyone to do better, knowing how little use we made of our capacities. And most of us responded.

It was Anna Shaughnessy who introduced me to Henry David Thoreau. His *Walden* was not part of the course of study. (It still isn't, in most schools.) She asked whether I knew of this Massachusetts writer who'd lived only some 40 miles away, in Concord. I didn't. Without scaring me off by proclaiming how great he was, she said he had lived and died in obscurity. But not like some romantic poet in a dusty garret. He had done all kinds of work for a living—been a schoolteacher, surveyor, pencil-maker, gardener, carpenter, mason, lecturer, naturalist, as well as keeper of a personal journal into which he wrote two million words.

Living nearby, he often came to Worcester to visit with two of his closest friends. One was Harrison Blake, a teacher, and the other was Theophilus Brown, a tailor. Brown lived at 10 Chestnut Street, Blake at 3 Bowdoin Street. Brown was called the "Wit of Worcester," and his shop was the hangout for the local intelligentsia.

The two men organized lectures for Thoreau (later, reworked, these speeches became part of his books) which he gave to small audiences in parlors or to bigger ones in Brinley Hall and even in City Hall.

I think the last time Thoreau spoke in Worcester was on November 3, 1859, at Washburn Hall. It was his "Plea for Captain John Brown," who had been captured during the raid on Harper's Ferry where he hoped to strike a blow against slavery. Thoreau, long an abolitionist and whose home was a hideout for fugitive slaves, wanted to explain the meaning of the sensational event and to celebrate John Brown's courage and his devotion to the cause of black freedom. The Worcester audience responded warmly to his speech.

"Thoreau was born in 1817, about a hundred years before you," Miss Shaughnessy said. "But I think, when you read him, you'll find his ideas, his way of looking at life, will mean as much to you as if he were born yesterday."

So I started on a copy of *Walden* that I borrowed from her. I found it hard going at first. But soon he drew me deep into the story of his two-year adventure living in his cabin at Walden Pond. He combined those two years into one, to give the book the rhythm and flow of the changing seasons. It opens with the building of the cabin in the spring, goes on to planting, weeding, and harvesting his bean patch, watching the ice-harvesting and ice-fishing in the winter, and closes with the return of spring.

Out of that pattern came his central symbol—rebirth and renewal, not only of the world of nature around us, but of our own inner development. Many years after my first encounter with Thoreau, when I was deeply troubled by the course my life was taking, I went back to *Walden* once more. On the last page, I read this passage:

Every one has heard the story which has gone the rounds of New England, of a strong and beautiful bug which came out of the dry leaf of an old table of apple-tree wood, which had stood in a farmer's kitchen for sixty years, first in Connecticut, and afterward in Massachusetts—from an egg deposited in the living tree many years earlier still, as appeared by counting the annual layers beyond it; which was heard gnawing out for several weeks, hatched perchance by the heat of an urn. Who does not feel his faith in a resurrection and immortality strengthened by hearing of this? Who knows what beautiful and winged life, whose egg has been buried for ages under many concentric layers of woodenness in the dead dry life of society, deposited at first in the alburnum of the green and living tree, which has gradually been converted into the semblance of its well-seasoned tomb—heard perchance gnawing out now for years by the astonished family of man, as they sat around the festive board—may unexpectedly come forth from amidst society's most trivial and handselled furniture, to enjoy its summer life at last!

As I finished reading those lines, I began to sob. The image of the bug emerging into life after all those years in its wooden tomb touched something deep in me. The tears poured out in relief. Feelings that had been frozen so long, melted in a rush. My wife, who had come running at the sound of crying, looked at me in amazement, then put her arms around me. I felt like one reborn.

I often went up to Miss Shaughnessy's desk after class—it was the last hour of the schoolday—to draw her out still more on the ideas that had excited me. This was the first of what would be two years with her, my junior and senior years at

Classical. I wasn't the only one. Another student—her name was Nina Hewitt—was often there beside me, just as eager to enjoy the play of Miss Shaughnessy's lively mind. Nina was a tall, slim, dark-haired girl, with huge amber eyes, quiet in manner, intense in feeling. We could tell at once that we shared many of the same interests. After a few sessions at the side of Miss Shaughnessy's desk, we asked her if she'd meet with a small group of students each week outside school and let us discuss some book we'd all read. She agreed, and Nina and I invited several others to join what we snobbishly called The Club. We met in the late afternoon at the teacher's house, and plunged deep into novels that were not on the school's reading list. There was always tea and cookies, but what we came to feast on was Miss Shaughnessy's brilliance.

It didn't take long for me to fall in love with Nina. At first I couldn't believe she returned my affection. She was one of "them," after all. She lived on the west side of town, and came from a middle-class Protestant family. Her father wrote editorials for one of the Worcester papers, and both he and her mother were college graduates. I felt that I could never ask her to my home. Partly because she was not Jewish and I had not forgotten that slap in the face from my mother. And partly because I wasn't sure how she'd take Ma and Pa, so different from what I imagined her folks were like.

I soon met them. Nina asked me to come to supper on a Saturday evening. They lived in a house of their own on a quiet, tree-lined street. Not a large house, but all their own. The street was paved, the sidewalk neatly bricked, the hedges clipped, the lawns smooth. Inside, lots of books and records on the shelves, prints on the walls, newspapers and magazines on the end tables. The talk at supper was about a biography someone was reading, or a summer vacation they'd enjoyed at Cape Cod, or politics, or something Mr. Hewitt was writing about.

They were good people, and when Nina kept inviting me over, always welcoming. I liked them, yet resented a little how sure of themselves they seemed to be. Taking it for granted this was their world, all wrapped up in a gift package. Once Mrs. Hewitt spoke of someone who was "just plain middle-class, like most of us." I wondered if she knew how people on our side of town lived.

Nina took me to her church on an occasional Sunday afternoon. Not to services, but to young people's socials. I'd glance around, to see whether any other Jews were there, wondering whether these people saw me as different somehow. Never a sign of that. Still, I felt strange sitting there—like a pretender.

It was better when we went somewhere on our own. One of our favorite places was the Worcester Art Museum, a handsome limestone building something like the Greek temples I'd seen on slides in our ancient history class. There were galleries of American and European art, and things from several other cultures. But almost always we hurried through those as we headed for our favorites, the French painters. Going into that room for the first time was like discovering what eyes are for. Those artists— Gauguin, Monet, Matisse—painted the most joyous pictures, filled with light and color. The Museum had only a few such works, but we hunted through the library for those oversize volumes reproducing in color the paintings of so many others— Pissarro, Renoir, van Gogh, Cézanne. . . . I felt like I'd been going around with dark glasses on and then suddenly someone tore them off and let me see the whole shining world. There were none of those battle scenes with heroic warriors you saw in other rooms, no castles or palaces or nymphs or goddesses. Just natural things—flowers, trees, fields of grain, rivers flowing through meadows, snow, mist, and *sun!* And when they painted people, it wasn't lords and ladies, but women at an ironing board, men playing cards, a farmer at work, people dancing, a girl doing her hair. And the colors they used! Not those glossy browns and blacks but yellow and orange and violet and blue and crimson and green.

On one of our Sundays in the Museum— it must have been the tenth time for us—I said how I wished one of these guys would paint the pond in Elm Park where we'd skated last winter. Or maybe even try those four cypresses standing out against the sky in Cheney's Field.

"What do you mean 'these guys,' " Nina said. "How about the women?" I'd forgotten. Miss Shaughnessy had just loaned Nina the new Virginia Woolf book, *A Room of One's Own,* and now she was always on the lookout for women who had done something special. I wouldn't have noticed that some of the pictures we liked were done by Berthe Morisot and Mary Cassatt, if she hadn't pointed that out. Once, in a book, we came upon one of my favorites, van Gogh's painting of a village postman. We studied it, the dabs and patches of color fell into place and the postman sprang to life. Then Nina said casually, "Think van Gogh would bother to paint a window cleaner?"

I had it coming. Only a few weeks before, Nina and I had planned to spend Friday afternoon and evening together, as we often did. As soon as school let out, we headed for the Museum. When we got to the corner of Main and Pleasant, we decided to drop into Easton's. It had the best soda fountain around, milkshakes so thick you could chew on them. We sat at the counter, ordering a strawberry shake for her and a chocolate for me.

While we were sipping on our straws, I happened to look past the fountain and saw Pa cleaning the big plate-glass window opposite. He was working from outside, wearing his old gray pants, a faded blue work-shirt, and a heavy pullover sweater Ma had knitted. His cap was jammed down to his eyes to keep the wind from snatching it off. He was totally absorbed in the job, never glancing into the store. Usually he was on his way home by this time; he must have had an extra rush job to do. I started chattering a blue streak to Nina, keeping my eyes away from Pa. When we finished, we paid, and started out. I would have taken the side door, but Nina headed rapidly for the front door, next to the window Pa was still working on. I couldn't do anything but follow. She headed left, in the Museum's direction. Again I followed. Just then Pa turned around. His eyes took us in. He had never seen Nina, but he knew me, all right.

"Hello, son," he said, in that kind of tentative voice you use when you aren't sure what's up. "Hi, Pa," I said, and then we were past him, and I hadn't stopped.

Two blocks in dead silence. Then, "So I've met your father at last."

I didn't know what to say.

"What's the matter with you? That *was* your father, wasn't it?"

I kicked an empty cigarette pack that had gotten in my way.

"He does look like you, a little. I mean, you look a little like him. The same gray-green eyes. Only his have a nice look. Yours look mean."

Now I'd found a trash basket that needed a good kick to get it off the curb.

"Aren't you going to say anything?"

"Nina," I said pleadingly, "I didn't see him at first."

"Maybe so, but you certainly did after. And you wouldn't even have said hello if he didn't speak to you first. And why didn't you introduce me? You just rushed past."

I could feel how hot my face was getting. "It's easy for you to act so superior. Your father doesn't have to clean up other people's dirt."

"But he's your father! You think a man's what he does for a living, only that, nothing more? He's as good as anybody else!"

"Easy for people to say, but do they really mean it? Look, my pa's a window cleaner, yours is a newspaper editor. Do people see them the same?"

"Of course they do, everybody does."

"They don't. And what's more, they don't feel that way about themselves. I mean, how can my father feel he's the same as yours?"

"What makes you so sure about your dad? Did you ever ask him? Did he ever say?"

"No, I just know it, that's all."

Or was it just the way *I* felt?

Of course we'd often talked about our families. She knew what Pa and Ma did, and about my brothers, and had asked me many times to tell her about where they came from, and how they got here. And I knew about her folks, and the long generations of Americans behind her. She'd suggested more than once that she'd like to see where I lived, and to meet my family. Without ever flatly saying no, I managed never to arrange it. And now she'd met Pa. She was appalled by my attempt to avoid it. And I was ashamed.

"Tyger Tyger, Burning Bright"

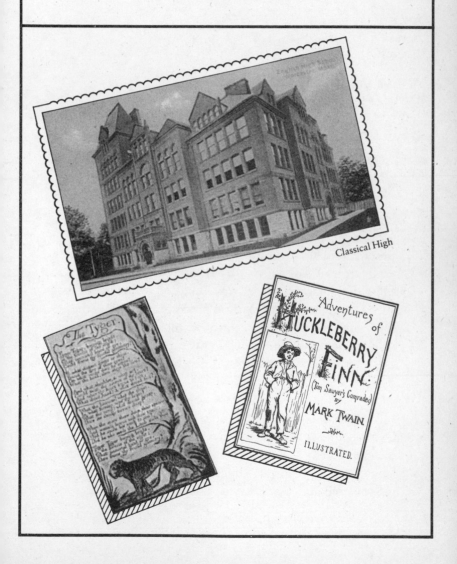

Classical High

I first encountered Adolf Hitler on the front page of the Worcester *Gazette*. Never having heard of him before, I would have paid his name no attention if it had not been linked to one word—*Jew*—in the news report.

Worcester was my world. I knew little of what went on beyond its borders. There was New York, of course, where my grandparents lived. There was Boston, with its beaches and tennis tournaments. There was Kingston with the Ludwigs' farm. There were other American places propelled into the news when some great athletic event or awful crime occurred there. The world beyond as reported in the press? A steady drizzle of wars and politics and business deals. Nothing I paid attention to.

Until a day in September 1930, when I first noticed the strange words *Nazi* and *Hitler* in the newspaper. I had begun to skim the foreign news because, at Classical High, Mr. Brennan was teaching us modern European history. The textbook demanded dreary hours of homework. But Mr. Brennan wanted more from us. He would bring up some piece of European news every day, and ask us to discuss what it meant. So you had to watch the papers to keep up with him.

On this particular day, something caught my eye in a report datelined from Germany. A hundred-odd members of Adolf Hitler's Nazi party had just been elected to the German legislature—the *Reichstag* they called it—and they had shown up for the first session wearing brown uniforms with a swastika on the sleeve and shouting, "*Deutschland erwache! Jude verrecke!*"

The paper obligingly explained what those foreign words meant: "Germany awake! Jews perish!"

It was those words that had leaped out at me from the small print. I wasn't looking for them. I didn't know they would be there. Still, I saw them as with a special sense, attuned to those three letters, J-E-W. My skin prickled when I saw that cry in the newspaper, "Jews perish!" I think whatever kind of Jew you are, believer or nonbeliever, doubter or atheist, you have absorbed somehow the knowledge that Jews live under threat. The very calendar that hangs in Jewish homes marking the anniversaries, many of which are catastrophes, followed only sometimes by salvation . . . Passover, to celebrate the escape from ancient enslavement under the Pharaohs . . . Purim, the time when Haman's plan to kill all the Jews of Persia had been foiled by Esther . . . Hanukkah, which marks the victory of the guerrilla fighters led by the Maccabees over the ruthless despot, Antiochus, who tried to suppress the religion and culture of the Jews . . . and the Ninth of Av, which is the fast-day for remembering, and mourning, the destruction of the Temple in Jerusalem, the first time by the Babylonians, the second time by the Romans . . .

No wonder, then, that an alarm bell rang whenever I saw or heard the word "Jew" in an unexpected setting. It might have been the sound of that word slashing into my ear while playing basketball in the gym. Or the sight of those three letters on the page of a book I was reading. But here on page one of the Worcester paper was something new to me. People elected to the German legislature, standing up in public, *now,* and shouting out that the Jews must die?

I shuddered. "This could never happen here, could it, Pa?" He looked at the story I pointed out, then smiled at me reassuringly. "Don't worry about it," he said. "Hitler and those crazy Nazis of his—they won't last long."

The next day, I asked Mr. Brennan about that piece of news. He had missed it. When he told me to tell it to the class, I was nervous. I got out the facts hurriedly, then stumbled over those German words (I had copied them down), and almost whispered the English of them. No one else in the class had noticed the story. Mr. Brennan said this was something that went back to the Versailles Treaty which ended the World War. (He didn't say "World War One," because World War Two hadn't happened yet, and who expected that it would?) "We'll find out later, what's been happening in Europe these last years," he said. "But don't take this news too seriously," looking at me. "There are always fanatics with insane ideas. People are too well-educated nowadays to follow a leader like this man Hitler. The Germans especially."

I wanted to believe him. And I guess I did. Who knew better?

Though I was a stranger to Germany, I felt something like a cousin to England. At least the England I learned about in the history and literature I read in school or out. In junior high, we'd been assigned *Ivanhoe.* The marvelous story Scott told captivated me. I loved Rebecca because of his warm portrayal of her. But all through the story other characters spoke of the Jews as usurers, liars, hypocrites, as covetous, contemptible, inhuman. I tried to ignore all that, but couldn't help feeling humiliated.

Charles Dickens I began reading on my own. *A Christmas Carol* was the first story, and though it wasn't my holiday, I wanted to share in its joyousness. A librarian told me to try *Oliver Twist.* "You'll love it," she said. I was drawn at once into the wanderings of little Oliver, the lost child, the rejected child, full of fear and hope. My sense of justice was quickened by Dickens' exposure of the vast cruelty and greed, the indifference which birthed the slums and the haunts of crime the story moves through.

But over everything fell the shadow of Fagin, that "villainous-looking . . . repulsive . . . greasy . . . shrivelled old Jew," to use Dickens' opening description of the master criminal into whose hands the tender and innocent little Oliver comes. The power of Dickens to create characters by an intense poetic simplification made the anti-Semitic caricature all the more horrifying. I remember hurrying my eyes over those pages in which he appeared, anxious to get on to passages less painful to me as a Jew.

I quickly saw in the novel that there were Christians, too, who were vicious, like the brutal Bill Sikes. But Oliver and all the other good people were Christians. They far outweighed the Sikes character. And the fact that Sikes was a villain had nothing to do with his being a Christian. In the case of Fagin, however, his villainy was made identical with his Jewishness. To be a Jew, the reader could only conclude, is to be a villain.

When I got to Miss Shaughnessy's English courses, we read a lot of Shakespeare: the sonnets, *Macbeth, Othello, Hamlet. The Merchant of Venice* was the first play we studied. Miss Shaughnessy said she had mixed feelings about taking this up. First, we had to, because it was required. Second, it had great poetry.

But third, the characterization of Shylock was anti-Semitic, she went on, though she had seen one or two actors perform it on the stage in a way that drew sympathy for Shylock.

Then she went on to tell us something of the background to the view of Jews in Shakespeare's day. She spoke of the way the Church and the State worked together in medieval times to make the Jews outcasts. How the Jews were shut off from farming the land, and banned from the Christian guilds, too, so they could no longer practice these crafts and trades, and how they were forced to become merchants and moneylenders. Then, as business in each country of Europe developed and expanded, Jews who had pioneered in business were restricted to smaller and smaller roles. And when they were no longer considered essential, she said, their Christian rivals called them greedy, miserly, heartless—and took over their functions themselves. Shylock, she said, has to be looked at in the light of that history.

After that, we were able to read the play and enjoy the superb lines, the imagery and rhythm, the dramatic structure, without, I thought, letting it poison our minds.

Those years—the Twenties and early Thirties—were the time of a great generation of American writers. William Faulkner, Ernest Hemingway, Sinclair Lewis, Willa Cather, Scott Fitzgerald, Theodore Dreiser, Eugene O'Neill. Their early work and some of their best work appeared month after month. Yet we did not hear about them in school. (Except through conversations with Anna Shaughnessy.) The curriculum was frozen in 18th- and 19th-century England and America. Dickens, Thackeray, George Eliot, Thomas Hardy: it was their novels we studied. When it came to poetry, we memorized big swatches of Milton, many passages from Keats and Shelley and Byron and

Wordsworth, whose romantic lines seemed so thrilling. Weeks and weeks went into long poems by Tennyson. Yet what I remember best are those lines of William Blake's:

> *Tyger Tyger, burning bright,*
> *In the forests of the night:*
> *What immortal hand or eye,*
> *Could frame thy fearful symmetry?*

I did not understand much of Blake or his visions, but sensed a secret buried in his singing language and the images he conjured up.

I did not find out till long after that possibly what triggered Blake's awe-inspired questions was a boyhood experience. Three tigers were on view in the Tower of London. Admission to the spectacle was three pence—or a cat or a dog to be fed to the tigers.

Essays were taken more seriously then as a form of literature. We read the Roger de Coverley papers, a little of Samuel Johnson, Burke's speeches, Lamb's essays. I liked much of what we took up, but I wish they had mixed in a bit of H. L. Mencken, whose cutting satire in the *American Mercury* I was reading.

Clearly the English writers were supreme, judging by the attention paid them in class. Americans were included, but not many. We read Longfellow's "Miles Standish" and "Hiawatha" and "Evangeline" and Whittier's "Snow-Bound," but none of his antislavery poems, which I discovered by myself soon after. As for Walt Whitman, nothing of the magnificent *Leaves of Grass*, only the wretched "O Captain, My Captain." Here again, I bought a one-volume edition of *Leaves* and have it to this day. These, mixed with a dash of Emerson's poems and essays, Hawthorne's *The House of Seven Gables,* and barely a nod to Thoreau, about whom long after I was to write two books. The closest we came to the 20th century was Stephen Crane's *The Red Badge of Courage.*

Mark Twain? We didn't read him in school. *Huckleberry Finn* had appeared only 30 years before I was born, and Twain himself had died only five years before. Which may have ruled him out as being too modern. Educators seemed to believe that a writer had to be dead an awfully long time before his ghost could pass through the classroom door. Besides, *Huck* had been removed from the children's shelves of both the Brooklyn Public Library and the Concord Library in Massachusetts because they said it was "morally injurious to the young." When I read it on my own, I was delighted with the language, with Huck's juicy talk as he tells the story. It was so daringly different from the formal prose of everything we were reading in class. But not what we were reading out of school. I had just finished Hemingway's new novel, *A Farewell to Arms,* and could see why he said, "All modern American literature comes from one book by Mark Twain called *Huckleberry Finn.*"

Yet though so little of what we read in school came directly out of our own time, I do not regret it. It led me beyond familiar boundaries. It opened me to the playfulness of language. I began to see that literature offers a way to live better, to breathe more freely, to discover new energies in myself. Surprise, delight, direction, all these are the strength of books. And best of all, the longer I live, the truer it is that books do not age, the way I do. They continue to speak, long after the writers and the readers of their own time are gone.

A Radical Tradition

ANTI-SLAVERY LECTURES.
1854-5.

THE OFFICERS OF THE

WORCESTER CITY
ANTI-SLAVERY SOCIETY,

HAVE THE PLEASURE OF ANNOUNCING THE FOLLOWING:

COURSE OF LECTURES,

TO BE DELIVERED ON

SUCCESSIVE FRIDAY EVENINGS,

AT THE

CITY HALL.

Nov. 24—CHARLES SUMNER, of Boston

Dec 1—JOHN PIERPONT, of Medford. (a Poem.)

   8—SALMON P. CHASE, of Cincinnati, Ohio

  15—(Omitted, to accommodate the Mechanics Association).

  29—(Wednesday.)—JOHN P. HALE, of New York

  29—CASSIUS M. CLAY, of Kentucky,

Jan 5—THEODORE PARKER, of Boston.

   8—(Monday.)—HENRY WARD BEECHER, of Brooklyn, N.Y.

  19—SAMUEL J. MAY, of Syracuse, N. Y.

  26—RALPH WALDO EMERSON, of Concord

Feb 2—LUCY STONE, (probably,) West Brookfield.

   9—N. P. BANKS, of Waltham.

  16—WILLIAM W. BROWN, recently from England

March 2—DAVID WILMOT, of Towanda, Pa

SINGLE TICKETS, 10 Cts.,

Packages of 10, to be used at any Lecture, 80 Cents

For Sale at the Bookstores, and at the Door.

Lectures Commence at 7 1-2 o'clock P. M

T. W. HIGGINSON, President

JOSEPH A. HOWLAND, Sec'y.

Abby Kelley

I think it was the antislavery poets who first made me conscious of a terrible injustice at the root of American life. When I read Walt Whitman's "Song of Myself," I came across these lines:

I am the hounded slave, I wince at the bite of the dogs . . .
I clutch the rails of the fence, my gore drips . . .
Agonies are one of my changes of garments,
I do not ask the wounded person how he feels, I myself
    become the wounded person.

There had been no black children in the schools I went to. Nor do I recall seeing black people on the streets of Worcester where I walked, or hearing about them in the newspapers I read. Invisible? Almost, though they were about 1% of the local population. They had lived in Worcester since the early 1700s. Some of the colonial families owned slaves. But free blacks, too, lived in Worcester, among them a Minute Man who had fought the Redcoats. Some of the fugitive slaves who found freedom in the town settled on what came to be known as Liberty Street, off Belmont. But it was not out of personal experience that I responded to Whitman. Let's say my mind was a blank page on this subject. Until Whitman wrote on it. And then James Russell Lowell, with his indictment of whites who failed to protest slavery:

> *They are slaves who fear to speak*
> *For the fallen and the weak ...*
> *They are slaves who dare not be*
> *In the right with two or three.*

And Whittier. I had known him for "Snow-Bound," that lyrical and intense picture of New England country life, a poem I remembered instantly, long after, when I first saw the paintings of Grandma Moses. The militant Quaker's poems proved to me that words had consequences. For himself: four times, Whittier's life had been endangered by pro-slavery mobs. And for millions of others: no other writer did so much to rouse public opinion against slavery.

Not content with the few bits of Whittier in my school anthology, I scoured secondhand bookshops until I found a volume of his antislavery poems. There I came across "The Rendition," a poem he wrote when Anthony Burns, a runaway slave from Virginia, was captured in Boston in 1854, and an attempt then made to free him led by Worcester men.

It sounded like an enormously exciting moment in history, yet it was absent from the pages of the textbooks. Not that the abolitionist movement was ignored, but its treatment was so brief, so dry, so general, that it never stirred the blood. When I asked Mr. Brennan about the Burns story after history class, he knew what I was talking about. Pleased to have an eager student, he sent me to the public library with a list of references I could look up. "It's Worcester history, too," he said. "When you find out why that is, tell us about it."

Higginson, Thomas Wentworth, was the name at the top of the list. Anything by or about him, Mr. Brennan had said. I found volumes of his letters, journals and essays, and the story of his leadership of a black regiment in the Civil War. Born in Cambridge, of an old Puritan family, he came to Worcester in 1852 when he was almost 30, to be the pastor of the new Free Church. Worcester's radicals had just united in an independent congregation and they picked this tall, handsome idealist to be their preacher. The town was at the heart of antislavery feeling in Massachusetts. It was the trading center for many independent-minded small farmers. In the new shoe factories springing up, workers read abolitionist pamphlets aloud to each other. "Radicalism went into the smell of shoe leather," said Higginson.

An abolitionist stronghold, Worcester was a key station on the Underground Railroad. Many an escaped slave en route to Canada was welcomed into citizens' homes. And many others, liking the town's spirit, decided to stay, relying on their fellow citizens to protect them from slave-catchers.

As early as 1767, the town had urged the province to put an end to the "unChristian practice" of slavery. The Free Soil Party was born in Worcester in 1848, pledging to resist the spread of slavery to the territories.

Higginson soon learned that Worcester was a "seething center of all the reforms," as he put it. And not the least of them women's rights. Early on, women had formed female wings of the antislavery societies, and done great work for the cause. But when some of them began to speak to mixed audiences, at first in parlors, then in churches, and finally in crowded lecture halls, they met the powerful prejudice against women. Many objections were raised to the "female orators." It was "highly improper" and "indecent" for them to speak before men. The women did not back down. Their struggle for equality in the abolition movement was a crucial step in the fight for women's rights. A Worcester woman, Abby Kelley, flung the boldest challenge to the ancient way of thinking. By her mid-twenties, she was sure that "to improve mankind" was "the only object worth living for." A tall woman with a trumpeting voice, she committed herself to reform without regard for her health, her reputation, or her personal safety. As a Quaker, she believed in nonviolent resistance to evil.

So successful was her first public speech that the abolitionists urged her to become a traveling lecturer for them. Her family tried to talk her out of it, but she stood fast and began a long and fiery career as an agitator. When she married another radical, Stephen S. Foster, she went back to Worcester where they bought a farm in the Tatnuck district. It became a haven for fugitive slaves.

Second only to the fight for black freedom was Abby's devotion to women's rights. She helped prepare the first national women's rights convention, held in Worcester in 1850, and Higginson signed the call for it. Both Abby and Stephen gave speeches to a thousand delegates assembled from 11 states. A year later, at the second women's rights convention, also held in Worcester, she made a major address. Abby became an inspiration and friend to the younger women—Elizabeth Cady Stanton and Susan B. Anthony—who would lead the movement.

But now Abby, Stephen, Higginson, and many other Worcester reformers became caught up in the mounting agitation against the Fugitive Slave Law of 1850. Abby and Stephen had built a secret vault into their cellar which could be reached only by a trapdoor from the room above. So many runaways hid with Abby and Stephen that their place became known as Liberty Farm.

The Fugitive Slave Law threatened to wreck the whole Underground Railroad. It laid much stiffer fines and prison sentences upon those caught assisting the fugitives, and raised the rewards of those catching them. Many abolitionists had pledged themselves not to use violence, even in self-defense. But the law was so weighted in favor of the slaveholders and so increased the danger even to free blacks in the North that men like Frederick Douglass abandoned their nonresistance and began to support blacks arming themselves. Still, nonresisters like Abby insisted that abolitionists should rely only on moral force, not physical force. Only the right means would secure the right ends, she argued.

Worcester abolitionists figured large in the most famous attempt to rescue a fugitive slave—the subject of Whittier's poem. It happened in May 1854. The ex-slave, Anthony Burns, was arrested and placed under guard in the Boston courthouse at the request of his former master, Colonel Suttle of Virginia. The news spread rapidly through the state. Three abolitionist lawyers appeared the next morning to persuade the court to postpone a hearing for a few days. That gave Higginson and Martin Stowell, his fellow townsman, a chance to plan their strategy. Friday night, Faneuil Hall overflowed with angry citizens gathered to protest Burns's arrest. The aim was to use the meeting to draw attention away from the courthouse, while a band of abolitionists would storm the building to free Burns.

On the platform at Faneuil Hall that night, a man cried out, "When we go from this Cradle of Liberty, let us go to the tomb of liberty—the courthouse!" That was to have been the signal for the crowd to burst out of the hall and head for Court Square, where Higginson and Martin Stowell together with Lewis Hayden, a prominent Boston black, were already leading a score of abolitionists in battering down the door of the courthouse to rescue Burns. But the abolitionists on the platform somehow failed to pick up the signal, and only a few people ran to the square to support the assault. Within the courthouse, constables and deputies were ready with pistols and clubs. Higginson was clubbed on the head and, in the scuffle, one of the deputies was killed. It was the first drop of blood shed in a fugitive-slave rescue case, a proof to some that war over slavery had begun. A police squad rushed up, and the abolitionists were soon routed. Many were arrested, Higginson and Stowell among them. (The indictments were later quashed, however.)

When news of the failed attempt was flashed throughout the state, Stephen Foster organized 800 Worcester men to hurry on a special train to Boston, where they were joined by similar protesters from all over Massachusetts.

The armed power of the government assembled in Boston was now so forbidding that the friends of freedom despaired of freeing Burns by force or by legal means. Over the weekend, they raised $1,200 and tried to purchase his freedom. But the U.S. Attorney refused to permit it. The refugee, in accord with the Fugitive Slave law, must be returned to Virginia, he said.

When Burns came to trial on Monday, police and soldiers surrounded the courthouse, guarded every door and window, and lined the staircase leading to the courtroom. The judge ruled in favor of the slaveholder. The day Burns was ordered back into slavery, police, Marines, lancers, dragoons, infantry, and cannon stood ready to prevent any last-minute rescue effort. Surrounded by thousands of armed men, Burns marched to the dockside through streets lined by 50,000 people, who were booing, hissing, and crying "Shame" to his captors. As the ship sailed from the dock, the crowd kneeled in prayer.

Then in October, came another chance to defy the slaveholders' government. Asa Butman, a U.S. Marshal and a notorious slave-catcher, arrived in Worcester. Was he there to capture some fugitive slave? Or to collect evidence against Higginson and the others who had tried to rescue Anthony Burns? No one knew. The Worcester *Spy* announced the presence of "The Human Bloodhound" and warned blacks to beware of the kidnapper. Local blacks, who belonged to Worcester's Vigilance Committee, which had been set up to protect fugitives, issued a leaflet threatening to tar and feather Butman.

Stephen and others formed a guard around Butman's hotel to keep watch on his every movement all through the night. At 3 A.M., alarmed by the noise outside, Butman came to the door with a revolver in his hand. He was promptly arrested for carrying a concealed weapon. At the court in the morning, a huge crowd stood outside to watch Butman brought in for trial. As he passed in, several blacks rushed at him and knocked him down with a heavy blow on the head. Fearing a bloody riot, the officials begged the abolitionists to quiet the mob outside.

Only a fervent appeal by the young lawyer George Hoar calmed the crowd for a time. Stephen, Higginson, and a few other abolitionists stepped forth to escort Butman to the railroad station. It was all they could do to keep the crowd from tearing him apart. They got him safely to the station and locked Butman into the privy for safekeeping until the train was due. When the crowd's anger boiled higher, Higginson managed to smuggle Butman away in a hack after Butman solemnly promised he would never set foot in Worcester again. It was believers in nonviolence who saved him from a lynching. Worcester took special pleasure in thoroughly frightening a man who had frightened so many.

I gathered all this from books in the Worcester library and proudly passed it on to Mr. Brennan's class one day. Imagine my delight when I found that it was Higginson who launched the movement to establish Worcester's free public library where I spent so many happy hours. It seems he was the kind of man who knew that everything—institutions, people, government— could be made better if you only worked hard at it.

"What This Country Needs"

It was in my junior year at Classical—1931—that my father began to come home early more and more often. Factories had cut down production and laid off workers. Stores were boarded up. There were fewer and fewer windows to clean. Jobs, even the worst, were hard to find. The best my older brother, my mother, and I could do was to get part-time work that lasted briefly and paid poorly. I found a Saturday job in a store on Front Street that sold the cheapest shoes. For $2 I worked from 8 to 8. The owner would sweeten the pay envelope by a quarter if you could fool a poor customer into buying a damaged or outmoded pair. I saw how desperate he was to keep his store going, but I didn't have the heart to do that. I lasted a few months and was laid off when business got even worse.

I tried to help out at home by taking over the billing for Pa's work. He had made a barter deal with a small printer: his windows cleaned in return for Pa's billheads. They were small square slips of blue paper. Across the top was printed BENJAMIN MELTZER, WINDOWS CLEANED, and then the address and phone number. Pa had wanted to put in the rates per window, but Ma said, "No, let people ask. Put the figure down," she said, "and with our luck times will change and you'll be stuck with a low price."

"What makes you think times will get better?" Pa said. "Maybe I'll have to cut the price."

"How can a price be lower than 15 cents?"

I bent over the kitchen table and went on with the billing. "Mrs. Mayfield, 10 windows at 15¢ each, $1.50." That was a big and handsome old house. I'd noticed it out walking with Nina. It was on her side of town. How many hours did it take, I wondered, to clean all those antique windows with their small panes of glass? It used to be 24 windows, but when Pa had done them the time before, Mrs. Mayfield had announced she was not using the upstairs rooms any longer. Too expensive to heat. Pa was to do only the first floor from now on. I thought, even the rich are trying to scrimp.

It didn't take long to finish the bills. Each month it took less. Stores Pa had done for many years had gone out of business. Maybe a third of the offices in the downtown buildings were empty now. And a fearful number of people had taken to cleaning their own windows at home. Worse, just the other day, a neatly dressed man had knocked at our back door and asked politely if he could wash our windows in return for a meal. Ma said she laughed at first, then got mad and sent the man away. "I shouldn't have done that," she said, "at least I could have given him something to eat."

Sometimes, though less often now, when Pa had to work into the night on a special job, I'd take his supper to him. One evening, it was to the Wallace place, a huge mansion still lived in by the old man of the family who ran their shoe factory. They had never left their large estate for the better side of town. I toted a brown bag with sandwiches, soup in one thermos and coffee in another. Walking through the dark streets, the voices of Amos and Andy on the radio followed me from house to house. I passed a big lot where kids used to play ball. Spread over it now were the ruins of a Tom Thumb golf course. I turned left on Mohawk Street. Down the block, I saw the marquee of the Rialto. CIMARRON, it read, but that was the Western playing when the place shut down six months ago. On the corner was Himmel's cafeteria. ALL THE FOOD YOU WANT TO EAT FOR 60¢ said the cardboard sign leaning against the dusty artificial fruit in the window. Next door was an empty store, and scribbled in soap on the glass, FOR RENT AT YOUR OWN PRICE.

Past the shopping district the big houses began. Rich families used to live in them, but long ago, even before I was born, they had moved to the west side. Their homes were chopped up into small apartments now, and the yards were full of junk.

Junk—that was the sign of the times. Factories junked, jobs junked, people junked. I was 15 then, and the Depression was in its second year. At home, a sour unease, like a noxious gas, hung in the air. Oh, we managed to eat. Ma could make do with almost anything. Food was cheap then, and the Depression drove prices even lower. At the corner grocery, eggs were 19¢ a dozen; lettuce, a nickel a head; whole-wheat bread, a nickle a loaf; bananas, 8¢ a dozen; mackerel, two pounds for a quarter; beef, 11¢ a pound; tomato sauce, 3 cans for 19¢. Cheap enough? But if you'd been out of work for months, you didn't have the pennies and nickels and dimes it took to buy anything.

As winter came on, crews of jobless men were given temporary work by the city, harvesting ice on Lake Quinsigamond. A woman on our street who had been working at the phone company for years was fired because her husband had a job. So were 20 other married women. In The Club, we were reading Carl Sandburg's poems. Miss Shaughnessy showed us a story in the *Gazette* quoting Herbert Hoover. The President had said, "What this country needs is a great poem. Something to lift people out of fear and selfishness. . . . Sometimes a great poem can do more than legislation."

Miss Shaughnessy paused, and looked up. "Well?" There was an angry outburst from my classmate Al. "A fine thing to have a President recognize poetry," he said, "but a poem can't feed the hungry. Does he care a cent for what hard times are doing to people? A chicken in every pot, he promised it, two cars in every garage!" It took a while till we got back to Sandburg. And then we saw that though a poem can't feed the hungry, it can condemn hypocrisy. It was the beginning of my love for Sandburg's passionate poems of protest.

A few weeks later, I was at Nina's for supper. Her father was late; he'd been traveling around the state all week to see what was going on in the mill towns. He showed up around eight, wouldn't eat anything, said he didn't feel hungry. He was a very tall man, and skinny as a broomstick. He was younger than my father, I knew, but while Pa's hair was still brown, Mr. Hewitt's was white. He had smoke-blue eyes, a nose that seemed to have been broken at one time, a wide mouth that laughed easily. His voice was rumbly, and though he talked fast, you didn't miss a word. Nina, who sometimes watched him when he worked on his editorials at home, said he wrote just as fast as he talked.

"How was the trip, Tom?" Mrs. Hewitt asked. "You're some writer. All we got was a measly postcard."

He told v it was awful, that we didn't know the half of it. If we thought things were bad in Worcester, the way people lived in those one-industry towns. . . . He shook his head. "It's one thing to sit in the office and write neat little analyses of economic data. God, but when you *see* what's happening!"

It had been his own idea to take a look. His publisher wasn't happy about it. Plenty of reporters to send out; why an editorial writer? But finally let him go. Pressed for time, he had stuck to the textile and shoe centers.

Even before Wall Street went smash, the mill workers lived practically from hand to mouth, he said. But now? Two out of five textile workers were out of work. Jobless for years, many of them, and those working had only one or two days a week. How could a man support his family, or just himself, on less than ten dollars a week? In the shoe towns, it was even worse, he said. Two out of three jobless.

"Know what I found to be the biggest industry in Lowell? Charity. Every third or fourth store in that city is vacant. In the tenement districts, I saw whole blocks of empty houses, windows broken, doors smashed, walls caving in, rats running wild. People just up and moved away—where to, who knows? Downtown the only busy store is the five-and-ten. Butchers told me all they sell is tripe and soup bones. Merchants run at a loss, caught in a trap. People owe them so much for years back, they fear that if they close shop they'll never see the debts paid. Yet if they stay open, things may get even worse."

He had talked to doctors. They couldn't collect their fees. Over half their patients were charity. Dentists told him that about all they do is yank teeth out. People can't afford dental care and stay away until it's too painful to go on.

"I never felt so desolate, walking those streets. Shabby men leaning against the brick walls, or standing on street corners, silent men in torn overcoats or sweaters, feet poking out of broken shoes. Sunken eyes in gray faces. Try to talk to them and they shuffle away."

We were silent, around the table. I couldn't look at him. There was so much pain in his voice.

"Three days was all I could take of that town. Then I tried Lawrence. The woolen mills are still open, but only for spurts of production. I went there on Sunday and got up before daybreak to watch the mills open Monday morning. Hundreds and hundreds of men and women were in the streets, moving toward the mills. But not to work, only to beg for work. They check in every Monday to see if the foreman can promise a day or two that week. I learned many have been doing this for months, and some for over a year. One woman said to me, 'I don't know nothing, only I got no job. No job, no job.' She kept saying it over and over. After a while I noticed a funny pattern. Men standing around, just waiting, would do the same thing—clap their hands two or three times, stop, than after a while do it again. It was a way to act busy. And then the people mumbling to themselves . . ." His voice trailed off.

"What's going to happen, Tom? It scares me . . ."

"I don't know," he said. In Fall River, it was just about as dead. He talked to a reporter who told him that for several weeks now a group of men, 15 or 20 of them, had been going into chain grocery stores and asking for credit. When the clerk said it was cash only, they told him to move away, they didn't want to hurt him, but they had to eat. Then they'd fill a bag with food and go out.

"Strangely," Mr. Hewitt said, "the stores don't call the police. That'd put the story on page one. And the company figures the fewer people who know about it, the better, or other folks would get the same idea. The paper found out what was going on, but it decided not to print it for the same reason."

"What if that kind of thing spreads," I said. "Everything will fall apart. But then, maybe Hoover would do something about it!"

"It *is* falling apart. Maynard, Housatonic, Haverhill, New

Bedford," ticking them off on his fingers, "they're all disaster areas. But the shoe towns? No better. If anything, the shoe manufacturers are the worst bunch. Always been out for the fastest dollar, the highest profit, and to hell with their workers, the public, or anyone else."

It made me think of the Wallace factory. Pa cleaned the windows in both the factory and the old man's house. Just a few weeks ago, Wallace had said he expected Pa to do his home for nothing, if he wanted to keep doing the factory. Pa had agreed, which made Ma mad as hell.

"What about the Wallace factory?" I said. "Are things the same there?"

"Well, they're not johnny-come-lately, like some of the other shoe firms. That mill's been here for many generations. But Wallace has been laying off men who worked for him 30 to 35 years. One of those old-timers told me he had practically nothing to fall back on during a layoff. He was half ashamed and half mad. Ashamed because he couldn't take care of his family, mad because they'd let Wallace get away with such low wages all this time, he couldn't put a dime in the bank."

"Are you going to write about it, Dad?"

Mr. Hewitt got up, walked to the parlor window, stood there looking out at the tall trees arching over the quiet street. "I don't know," he said.

"What do you mean, Dad? Wasn't that the purpose of your trip?"

He didn't turn around. "Yes," he said. "But the way I feel . . ."

"I think we know how you feel, Tom," Mrs. Hewitt said. "Isn't that what you'd write about?"

"That's just it, Carrie. I'm not sure how I feel. Or rather, what to say about how I feel."

"Well," she said, "it would be the first time you didn't know what to say!"

He didn't smile. "Carrie," he said, "I'm worn out. I'm going to bed. How about you?"

"In a minute, Tom. You two know where the refrigerator is," turning to us. "Help yourselves when the supper wears off. Don't stay up too late, Nina." She smiled at me and followed Mr. Hewitt up.

It was going on eleven now. If I didn't leave soon, the trolleys wouldn't be running and I'd have to walk miles to get home. Nina moved over to the sofa and I sat down beside her.

"I like your father," I said, "your mother, and even you." And I started kissing her. She kissed back, slow, tender kisses. Then we were leaning back and pretty soon lying down. The lights were out in the upstairs hall and it felt like we were in a home of our own. I took out the clasp that held her long hair and it came down over her shoulders in a silken black wave. I loved to bury my face in its softness. We turned off the parlor lights except for a small table lamp in the farthest corner. I could barely see her face in the dark. The whole length of her body was close against mine. I don't know how long we were there, whispering and stroking each other. We'd never done more. I don't know why. It was as though we'd reached a place that we didn't want to go beyond. Not yet. I heard a noise upstairs and then Mrs. Hewitt called out, "You'll miss the last trolley."

I got up and went to the kitchen. I gulped down a glass of milk and Nina stuffed an apple in my pocket. We kissed at the door. I walked to the next corner where the trolley stopped. The streets were deserted. I looked at the time—an old pocket-watch Pa had given me—and realized the last car had gone half an hour ago. It was cold. The leaves of the maples were red and yellow in the gutter. I jumped into a mound of them someone had raked together, punted them like a football, and started out. Above, through the half-bare branches, I could see the stars following me home.

Tragic Towns

FUND SHORTAGE BIG HANDICAP TO WORK HE..

Add 75 to ...
350 ...

GROUP REPORTS 12 JOBS FOUND

Net Result of 28,000 Circulars and Appeals to Clergy

1000 IN DIRE NEED

Committee Members Point to Necessity of City Loan

Although 28,000 circulars were d...
tributed to ... hildren

21 BOOTHS FOR IDLE TO ENROLL TO OPEN TODAY

70 Volunteers and Eight Supervisors in Charge Of Work

WILL CHECK LISTS

Hildreth Says Names of Totally Unemployed Will Be Taken

300 GIVE WORK FOR CITY RELIEF

Engaged in Cutting Brush And Raking Leaves In Parks

HAVE DEPENDENTS

Eight inches of snow fell toward the end of that year of 1931. A blessing for the unemployed. The city hired men with dependent families to clear the streets. Letters in the papers asked why Washington didn't do something to feed the hungry. But President Hoover said a relief program would only tear up the country's roots.

Coming home from school one day, I passed the common behind City Hall and heard loud voices in a rhythmic chant. I saw about 75 men and women, ringed by many police, walking in a large circle. The demonstrators carried hand-lettered signs calling for free coal, electricity, food, and clothing for needy families. I watched a young man break from the circle and mount a soapbox. It was Adam Silverberg, a neighbor of mine. A year older than I, he was a freshman at Clark University, one of Worcester's several colleges. He was a brilliant student, and I'd wondered why he hadn't tried for a scholarship elsewhere. "I don't want to go away," he said, "I've got plenty to do right here." He had joined a radical youth group, devoted to campaigning for jobs and relief for the unemployed. I stopped to hear what Adam would say. As the pickets fell silent, he yelled up toward the windows of Mayor O'Hara's office, "Put us to work! There are 12,000 unemployed people in Worcester, and you offer us three jobs shoveling snow! We don't ask for charity. We want work! If the capitalists won't give us jobs, give us the means to live!"

The police listened quietly. When Adam stopped, the pickets began to move off. He got down from the soapbox and was carrying it away when he spotted me off on the side. "Hey, why didn't you join in?" I said nothing. "Well, maybe next time? Here, take this and read it," handing me a leaflet. He hurried off to catch up with the pickets. I drifted away.

Adam had tried to involve me before this. A few months earlier he had loaned me his copy of *Living My Life,* the new autobiography of Emma Goldman. "A famous radical," Adam said. "More dangerous adventures then all those Nick Carters we used to swap. But hers *mean* something." I read how she had spent two years in prison for opposing military conscription in the World War, and then had been deported. Adam had whetted my curiosity by telling me she and her lover, Alexander Berkman, had run an ice-cream parlor on Providence Street, right here in Worcester, in 1892. That was the year of the great steel strike in Homestead, near Pittsburgh. Her book tells how she helped Berkman prepare to assassinate Henry Clay Frick, the steel magnate who refused to give an inch to the workers. Only lack of funds kept Emma from Berkman's side when the attempt was made. Frick survived, but Berkman disappeared for 14 years inside prison walls.

Soon after leaving Worcester, Emma herself served a year in jail for telling an audience of unemployed people in Brooklyn that "it was their sacred right" to take bread if they were starving and their demands for food were not met. When I read that, I thought of what Nina's father had said about the men in the textile towns who had just done exactly what Emma said was justified.

Much as I understood why Emma hated Frick, it troubled me that she wanted to kill him. She said she and Berkman meant to destroy Frick and thereby arouse the workers to revolt. But the outcome was neither. Frick lived on to become an even harsher enemy of labor. And the workers felt Berkman had only harmed their cause. They lost the strike, and their union was broken. Later, Emma wrote, she came to regret the attempt on Frick's life and to change her mind about terrorism:

> I feel violence in whatever form never has and probably never will bring constructive results. . . . Never again had I anything directly to do with an act of violence. . . . In the zeal of fanaticism I had believed that the end justifies the means. It took years of experience and suffering to emancipate myself from the mad idea. . . . I could never again participate in or approve of methods that jeopardized innocent lives.

I read Adam's leaflet at home. It urged people to pressure Congress for government relief, work projects, and unemployment insurance. It made sense, I thought. But I wasn't ready to do much about it. Then, two weeks later, Joe Paulokonis, whose father worked for the sanitation department, told me that everyone working for the city had been asked to give a percentage of their pay to a fund for the unemployed. If they didn't, they'd get a pay cut. But that month there was no pay—not for the mayor or any of the other city workers. Worcester's treasury had gone dry.

Just before Christmas recess at school, the front pages reported that 1,500 hunger marchers had reached Washington and found the doors of the White House and the Capitol barred to them. Bill Miller told me that his father, who had worked on the railroad all his life, was being asked to take a ten percent pay cut. Would he? "Sure," said Bill. "It's that or a bunch of them being fired."

We didn't laugh when City Hall announced on Christmas Eve that 26 more men would be given apple-selling posts. So many people were peddling apples on street corners that the Mayor had to regulate the trade. It was cold comfort to the apple merchants to see on page one of the *Telegram* that bankers were in trouble, too. Nine banks in the state closed as the year ended, including our own Bancroft Trust Company.

Then, on New Year's Day, 1932, I read the lead editorial in the *Telegram*. *Remember the year 1931 as a year of disaster*, it said. *The storm of depression which broke late in '29, which swept with cumulative force through 1930 and finally reached a crescendo of evil in 1931—that storm people will try to forget with the facility which human psychology gives for casting bad memories out of the mind. . . .*

Forget? What a Pollyanna conclusion! I knew Nina's father would never have written such nonsense. I'd been watching the paper for his reports on what he called the "tragic towns" of Massachusetts. I knew he'd finished the series. But why hadn't the articles appeared? I couldn't keep quiet any longer and asked Nina. She said he'd taken them to the paper—and he'd had them thrown right back in his face. Things were bad enough already, the publisher said. No need to give the gory details. It would only hurt business, and what good would that do anybody?

Nina said her dad was disgusted at first, then he got mad. No one was going to shut him up. If his own paper wouldn't print the story, maybe someone else would. So he had just reworked the series into one long article, and mailed it off to *Harper's* magazine. One day passed. Two. Three. Then, on the fourth day, I walked Nina home from school, to find her mother in wild excitement. "They've taken it! They've taken it! *Harper's* just phoned. They say Tom's piece is so powerful and so important they've ripped out something else to make room for it in the issue about to go to press!"

I never saw anybody so excited. We all were. Mr. Hewitt had been on the paper for 20 years, but he'd never tried for anything bigger. Now he'd be in one of the best national magazines. Influential people read it. Maybe something would be done. Things were happening!

They sure were!

The article caused a terrific uproar in all the towns described. The story became front-page news (even his own paper had to mention it) and the subject of dozens of editorials around the country. But many of them, especially within the state, were not what he expected. No, the editorials denounced the magazine and attacked Mr. Hewitt. They said if he wasn't a liar, he was certainly a sick man, hard to tell which. Or maybe he was a Communist? City councils passed resolutions attacking the article, the magazine, and Nina's father. A Lowell newspaper said that "the men and women of Lowell are as good, as honorable, as clean and decent as any people within the limits of any similar city in America, or in any country of the world. Their thrift, industry and self-respect are all that they should be."

But what did that have to do with the case? The thing was, what were those towns doing to create jobs, or to help starving people? Nothing, nothing at all. All they could think of was to attack the messenger who brought the bad news.

It was Saturday noon. I'd gotten up early so as to do my homework before going over to the west side to pick up Nina.

The phone rang. "Guess what," she said, "Dad's fired."

"Quit kidding."

"No, I mean it. The paper fired him, last night."

I could tell from her voice that she couldn't quite believe it.

"I'll be right over," I said.

When I rang their bell, Mr. Hewitt came to the door. "Hello," he said. He looked the same, except that he was in his bathrobe. I never saw him that way before. I felt I had to say something. "Mr. Hewitt," I said, "I heard . . ."

He waved his hand vaguely as if to say, it's nothing.

Nina came out and we started walking through the snow.

She told me what had happened. All those nasty editorials and resolutions were bad enough. But it was the mill owners who did it. They told the publisher he was keeping a Red on his payroll. When Mr. Hewitt heard that the first time, he laughed. But the publisher didn't. The paper had been in trouble because advertising was falling off badly. A list for layoffs had been drawn up. Mr. Hewitt had been there a lot longer than some others, who weren't let go. But that didn't matter when they fired him.

"What's going to happen now? I'm scared!"

I put my arm around her shoulders. "Don't worry," I said. "Your father will get something as good, even better, after that piece. I bet *Harper's* will take him on."

"They won't. I said the same thing and Dad said they have only a few editors and everything else is written by freelancers."

"How is he taking it?"

"Well, last night, when he came home and told us, he made jokes about it at first. 'Maybe the Communists will hire me,' he said. 'I can write their speeches for them.' But, by the time I went to bed, he was looking grim. This morning, I could hardly get a word of out of him. Mom's been telling him he'll get a job on another paper somewhere, but he keeps saying no, he likes it here, he was born and raised here, he doesn't want to leave."

Leave! That word chilled me. What would we do if she had to move? How, when, would we see each other?

When we got to Elm Park we sat down on one of the benches facing the pond. I felt cold and hugged Nina close. Her head rested on my shoulder. We didn't say anything for the longest time. The trees were bare, and the grass had turned brown. The ground felt hard underfoot. I watched two small boys testing the ice at the edge of the pond. A lone duck, who had forgotten to fly south, paddled slowly in the open water, leaving a tiny wake.

"Nina, what are you thinking?"

"Nothing. I don't want to think."

"You won't go away, will you?"

"I wish I could promise you . . ."

"Promise."

"All right, I promise." She turned her head up and I bent to kiss her.

"Hey, look at those love bugs!" It was one of the kids by the pond.

We got up and started back to her house. It was hard to make the time go by. We listened to the radio, tried dancing to a record, flipped through an album of family pictures. Her folks were home. Mrs. Hewitt with a book in her lap, but not turning the pages, and Mr. Hewitt drifting from one room to another. They both seemed sunk inside themselves. Supper was cold cuts, and fits and starts of conversation. An hour later, I said I'd better go home. I thought maybe they'd rather be alone, the three of them. In the hallway, Nina kissed me so hard my teeth hurt.

A Pair of Stockings

Without waiting around to see if a local job would open up—there was only one other paper in town—Nina's father took to the road to find work. He covered New England first; nothing there. Then he drove out to the Midwest. His letters grew shorter and sadder as the days passed with no prospects. Most papers were laying off staff; some had closed down. Several weeks after he left, I could see Nina was even more worried about her father. She didn't like what his letters were saying. In the last one, he wrote he had a great idea. He had just read about how fish taken from the Arctic Sea froze stiff in the air. But when they were tossed into a bucket of warm water, they returned to life. Why couldn't that be done with me, he said. Somone could stow him away in the bottom of a refrigerator plant and when things get back to normal again, take him out and throw him into a hot bath. Now wouldn't that be a workable way of beating the Depression?

That letter made me feel terrible, too. It sounded like he was about ready to give up. I tried to assure Nina that he'd be all right. Only he might have to go even farther off to find a paper that needed him.

"I wish I could do something," she said. "Get a job so he won't feel so desperate. I'd quit school. But Mother won't hear of it. She's been looking for a job herself, and can't find one. Yet she keeps saying things aren't going to be this bad forever. She insists I've got to prepare for college. But what's the use if there won't be any jobs?"

I couldn't answer that.

At our house, everything seemed the same. Pa was home early very often. But then, several days running, Ma wasn't home when I got in from school. The first day, I thought nothing of it. Then I noticed she looked quite tired when she did come in around five. That was unusual. Ma had more energy than our whole basketball squad put together.

It was a day or two later that I found out something was going on. I was in the cellar to bank the fire in our furnace before going to bed. I squatted in front of it, roasting an apple over the coals, watching the skin turn brown and smelling the fragrant bubbling juices. Then I spotted a small suitcase on a shelf to the side. It was medium-blue with white trim, and it looked brand-new. I lifted it down. It didn't feel heavy. But there was something in it. The bag was locked. I shook it. No sound. Then I noticed there were initials stamped in one corner: M. M. Not me! It could only be "M. M." for Mary Meltzer.

I forgot about my apple and ran upstairs with the suitcase. Ma and Pa were sitting at the kitchen table drinking tea.

"Hey! Look at what I found near the furnace!" I held up the bag.

"Just put it right back where you got it," Ma said.

"Wait a minute," said Pa. "Did I ever see that before? Looks brand-new to me. You going somewhere, Mary?"

"Foolish! Where would I be going these days? It's a bag I had to get because it's such a good bargain."

"Bargain or not," Pa said, "who has money for it? Especially when we don't need it?" He'd picked up the bag now and was examining it. He noticed the initials.

"What's this? A bargain and they throw in gold initials too? Who's getting so fancy?"

Then he realized the bag wasn't empty.

"There's something inside," he announced.

"What could be inside, Ben? Don't be silly!"

"Enough of secrets," he said. "You tell us."

"I was going to tell you, but later, when it would all be worked out."

"What's to work out?"

Ma went to her purse and took out a little key. She turned the lock. It snapped open. The lid popped up. We leaned over to look. The suitcase was full of stockings, long filmy ones, all the same color, beige. I couldn't figure out what Ma would be doing with a mess of stockings.

Pa reached in and tossed the stockings high in the air. Ma grabbed at them, trying to keep them from falling on the floor. "Crazy! What are you doing? You'll get them all dirty!"

"What are *you* doing?" Pa said. "Don't tell me. I know."

He turned to me and as though Ma were not right there, he said, "She thinks I can't support this family. It's not enough for me to work. *She* has to work, too."

I didn't understand. "What's this about, Ma? Have you got a job?"

Before she could answer, Pa was at it again. "Some job!" he snorted. "A peddler. Door to door she goes, peddling her stockings with gold initials on them!"

"Why are you so mad, Pa? What's wrong with peddling?

People need something, you have it, so you sell it to them. Is there something wrong with that?"

"That's not the point," Pa said. "I'm working. I'm paying the bills. She has enough to do at home. She doesn't need to be running around the neighborhood begging people to buy from her."

"Ben, I'm only doing what has to be done. Winter's dragging on, we'll need more coal. The boys will need new clothes in the spring. And you, how many years is it that you've worn the same old overcoat?"

"I don't need anything!" said Pa.

"But you both worked before we came along," I said. "I know other kids' mothers are working. What's wrong with that?"

"Mary, did I mind when you worked before we had the children? Didn't we both work back in New York? But *now* is different, now I don't want you to!"

"No, now I *must!*"

"Mary! I say no. I don't want you climbing those stairs and ringing doorbells and begging people to buy a pair of stockings!"

"I am not the only one, Ben! There are women going house to house, women right in this neighborhood, with corsets and underwear and makeup and God knows what! And it isn't begging, it's selling!"

"To me it's begging. If they want stockings, let them go buy in a store."

"But I've tried that. They're not hiring, they're only firing. All you can get is to work on commission. They give you the suitcase, the initials, the stockings, and you go out and find the customers. What you sell, you get a percentage on."

"How much did you sell, Ma?"

"Enough."

"What's enough?" said Pa.

"I've only been doing it four afternoons. And I sold a pair, the third afternoon, it was. But I'll do better. I need to learn."

"Four afternoons," said Pa. "That's maybe 12, or 15 hours of climbing stairs and ringing doorbells. Remember, Mary, you are no spring chicken anymore. Kids can run upstairs all day, but not you. And if you sold one pair, maybe you made twenty cents?"

I knew what was troubling Pa. His pride was hurt. For Ma to step in and try to help was an open admission that he had failed. He should be able to support his family by himself. That was the man's job. He *was* supporting us, but Ma could see, we all could see, that the money coming in was shrinking by the day. She was a resourceful woman. She'd never sit and cry over hard times. If something had to be done, she would do it. And Pa knew that about her. He had to protest, but there was little force behind it. She was right. We needed her help. Pride be damned.

Ma peddled her stockings for months, never able to make it pay decently. The women whose doors she knocked on were all in our part of town. No one was doing well. What could they buy? How could they pay? Even the ten cents a week for a life insurance policy was too much for thousands of people. Then Ma tried another tack. She rented a tiny space in the Slater Building—the same one where Pa's work closet was—and arranged for a brother of hers in New York to send her a small shipment of dresses from his garment factory. She hung them on a rack and waited for customers to come. A few from her small circle of friends dropped in, picked over the rack, perhaps bought the cheapest dress for a few dollars, and left. She couldn't afford to advertise and she had no show window on the street. That venture, too, went down the drain.

I think now that if my mother had been given the chance to go to school in America, and to prepare herself for some skilled trade or a business or a profession, she would have made a success of it. But the odds were all against her. Yes, there were Alger-like heroes who rose from nothing to become rich and powerful. But how many of them were there? Innumerable others—the anonymous millions of immigrants—began life here with hope, but died without its ever being realized.

Seventeen

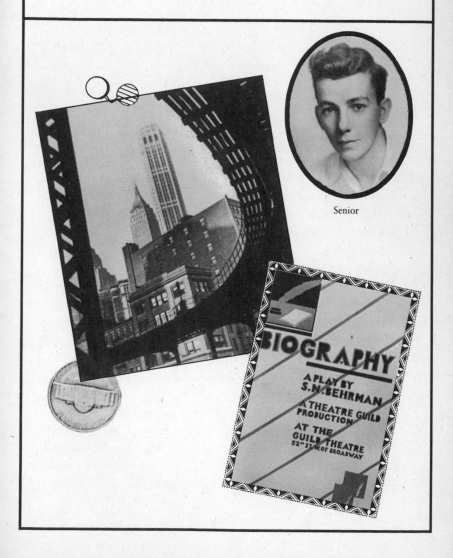

Senior

BIOGRAPHY
A PLAY BY
S. N. BEHRMAN
A THEATRE GUILD
PRODUCTION
AT THE
GUILD THEATRE
52ND ST. W. OF BROADWAY

That was my last winter in Worcester. At school, my senior year rolled on. A class dance, the basketball and hockey games, electioneering for office. No athlete, but a "word man," I began to take writing more seriously. I wrote for and edited the literary magazine, made the debating team and the yearbook board. Almost everyone talked of little else but getting into college. That's why they were at Classical. Many had little to worry about. Their families had money and had hung onto it, even during these bad times. If they had survived so far, they could pretty much choose their college. For the rest of us, from my side of the tracks, it wasn't that easy.

At first, I was drawn to a college that had a special aura for me. For the last couple of years, I had made a bit of money by posing for a Worcester painter. He sold only a few canvases, so to put bread on his table, he did illustrations for stories in slick magazines. When they called for a teenage boy, he asked me to come over and pose. It was fun to be in an artist's studio and see how he worked. He was swift and sure, and the sittings were never too drawn out to be tiring or boring. I learned Bill

Link was a graduate of the University of Virginia. The college Thomas Jefferson founded and designed, he said proudly, showing me pictures of the beautiful campus. But would they accept me, a Jew? Virginia, the South, aristocrats? It sounded scary. "They took me," Bill said, "and I'm a Jew. Not that they loved me," he added. "But I managed."

I talked it over with Miss Shaughnessy. She didn't discourage it, but neither was she enthusiastic. Then one day, she told me of a new experiment in progressive education about to be launched at Columbia University. The first class would start this fall of 1932. New College, it was called. Its aim was to prepare undergraduates for a teaching career, but in a wholly untraditional way. It would scrap the old method of grading through credits and adding up a score to see if you'd made it. There would be a small number of students and a faculty working closely with each one of them, a seminar system of study, periods of factory work off campus, experience on a southern farm, and a year of study abroad.

The idea was immensely appealing. Miss Shaughnessy had already been in touch with New College and assured me that promising students who needed aid would be granted a full scholarship and a campus job to help pay for board and room. I applied, was interviewed, and accepted. Pa said that somehow he would scrape up whatever I needed to make ends meet. (It turned out to be $5 a week.)

So things were looking up for me. And for Nina, too. Her mother had a part-time job now—if you can call it a job when you don't get paid. She was preparing luncheon in a women's club, and, in return, they gave her food for the family dinner. Not much, but it helped. So did a few dollars a week from Nina's father. He was working in Ohio. At first he didn't say what he was doing. But after they begged him to come home at least for a weekend so they could see him again, he wrote he couldn't because of his job. He was night janitor in a big apartment house. He worked 12 hours a shift, seven nights a week. He wasn't sure how long it would last. Into the spring, he thought. After that, he'd see.

When Nina read to me from that letter, I feared she would break into tears. But she didn't. She thought her father was something special. He hadn't quit; that was what mattered. She tucked the letter back into her jacket pocket. We'd been huddled over a fire we had built on the edge of Long Meadow. Feeling warm again, we got up and skated out on the ice. It was a huge marshland on the far edge of town which froze over in real cold weather. It made great skating. There was a crackling sound as the ice settled under our weight. Sometimes we passed over places where the water had run out beneath the ice and a hollow sound rumbled up. Going around a bend, we ran into a thin layer of snow on top of the ice. We stroked over it, our skates making a muffled sound, as though we were on woollen runners. Then suddenly we were on a space ridged like a washboard, and catching a snag, I let go of her hand and went sprawling. She knelt beside me and when she saw I was laughing, picked up some snow and rubbed it over my cheeks. I pushed aside the scarf wrapped over her head and, holding her face between my mittens, kissed the snow fringing her eyelashes, then her cold nose, then her warm mouth.

"Hey, you," she whispered.

"No need to whisper," I said; "nobody's here but us."

She stood up then, cupped her hands like a megaphone around her mouth, and yelled my name.

"It's me, O Lord," I said, looking up from the ice, "standing in the need of love."

Laughing, she reached down and yanked me to my feet. Now

the meadow was making a belching sound, as though the water beneath was heaving up against the ice. We began racing to the far end, Nina a little ahead, sweeping along with a lovely floating motion, leaning now to this side, then to that. She turned with the curve of the meadow, and we skated swiftly in a great arc back to where our fire had almost died out. We clumped off the ice and found some dry leaves and branches to revive the flames. A light wind had come up, blowing snow down from the trees in fine showers. Nina took off her scarf and her black hair shone with beautiful star-shaped crystals of snow. Above her head, red alder catkins dangled at the ends of twigs. It made me think of spring. A long way off.

Nina reached into a pocket and took out a winter apple. I split it into halves with the pressure of my thumbs, and we munched its pulpy whiteness.

"I have something to tell you," she said.

"What?"

"I'm going away to college in the fall."

I felt both bad and good, all mixed together. I had put off telling her about New College because things were so bleak for her at home. I'd thought she had no chance to go to college. Too, I felt unhappy about leaving her, and not seeing her any longer. Yet not so unhappy that I refused to go. (There were colleges in Worcester, after all, and I could have applied to them. But the desire to start something very new, on my own, was too strong to resist).

"Where?" I said.

"To Antioch—you know, in Ohio. Dad has a friend on the faculty, an old classmate. He talked to him about me, and found out that, with my grades, I could get a scholarship, and a job to help support me."

"That's great, Nina! I'm so glad for you!"

"But what about you?" she said. I told her, and it turned out that she had withheld the news from me for the same reason. I think we knew, somehow, that we were not ready to tie our lives together any more closely. We felt the pain of parting soon, but we shared the joy of a new life ahead, the great expectations of an unknown future.

We put out the fire, slung our skates over our shoulders, and started back to her house.

"I wonder," she said, "what we'll remember of this time, if we ever grow old."

One thing I remember is a pop tune we heard on the radio over and over again: "Brother, Can You Spare a Dime?"—the song I borrowed years later as the title of my book on the Depression. The poignant words and melody brought listeners to the edge of tears. The song thrust you into the sufferings of millions of people. It made you feel their pain, and if you, too, were living on the thin edge, it added to your bitterness.

Many writers were shaping into words the images of a country falling into ruin. I had begun reading *The Nation* and *The New Republic* in high school. Writers I admired were using their talents for special reporting in these weeklies. John Dos Passos, Erskine Caldwell, Langston Hughes, Sherwood Anderson, Edmund Wilson crisscrossed the country to go behind cold statistics and touch the anguish and desperation of real men and women after nearly three years of the Depression. How could this happen, they asked, in this, the richest country on earth, with the fattest acres, the tallest buildings, the mightiest machines, the biggest factories? Who is to blame?

Then Theodore Dreiser's name broke into the news: one of American's greatest writers, arrested in Kentucky as "a dangerous radical." This, just as The Club was discussing with Miss

Shaughnessy his novel *An American Tragedy*. The pathetic hero, Clyde Griffith, is convicted of murdering his pregnant sweetheart, yet Dreiser made us feel how false values and greed for wealth had overwhelmed the weak Clyde. Dreiser had gone down to the coal country of Kentucky to investigate the miserable conditions of the miners and the violence against them by the coal operators. The report of his findings aroused national anger.

As soon as the news stories from Kentucky appeared, Adam Silverberg wrote a leaflet about it, making the point that working people were being badly treated right here in Massachusetts, not only in Kentucky. And nothing was being done about it. He organized his friends to hand out the leaflets in the center of town. I took a batch from him, and stood on a street corner to pass them out. Some people reached eagerly for them, others turned away from my outstretched hand. What are they afraid of, I wondered. Learning facts? Having feelings? I'd read that Dreiser had grown up poor. Adam said, "I like a guy like that. He hasn't forgotten where he came from. He's using his knowledge to try to make people's lives better." He didn't hole up on Park Avenue to enjoy his money and fame, and to hell with everyone else. "You watch," Adam said, "he'll be an even better writer for seeing what he's seen, and doing what he's done."

Yes, writers could help people in trouble, using their power with words and the influence they had earned. After all, hadn't President Hoover said, "What this country needs is a great poem, something to lift people out of fear and selfishness. . . . Sometimes a great poem can do more than legislation." But people had reason to be fearful. One-fourth of the nation by this time in 1932 belonged to families with no regular income. And who were the selfish ones? Not the needy, but the wealthy businessmen who fought any attempt to raise their taxes so the hungry could be fed and the homeless housed.

One day in January, my father was cleaning the windows in a downtown restaurant when he noticed a flurry of excitement at a table nearby. A man had ordered oysters, salad, a steak, pie, ice cream, and coffee. After finishing his meal, he called the manager over and said, "Now you can put me in jail. This was my first meal in three days. I haven't got a dime."

In February, a young actress who had gone to Classical High and then to drama school committed suicide. She had gone to Broadway full of hope and ambition, but could not find even a walk-on role in a starving theater. She came home to Worcester, sat silently alone for weeks, then took a trolley car out to Lake Quigsigamond, chopped a hole in the ice, and drowned herself.

School straggled to a close. I did not stay till the last day of my senior year. An uncle in New York, in answer to my mother's appeal, had offered me a summer job in his dress factory. Come as early as you can, he wrote, so you can earn more money. Miss Shaughnessy got the principal to release me early in May.

I left home eagerly, yet reluctantly, too. I had hardly ever been away before. I knew this time it would be for keeps. Four years at New College were ahead, and then what? I appeared to be confident, to be sure of myself, to know what I wanted and where I was going. Inside, I was shaky, scared of being alone in New York, fearful of being so homesick I wouldn't be able to stick it out. But I couldn't reveal that to anyone. Certainly not to Pa and Ma, not to Miss Shaughnessy, not even to Nina. You're supposed to be grown up, now, I told myself, so act it! I said good-bye to my brothers, to Pa and Ma. Send home your dirty laundry, Ma said, and I'll mail it back clean. Adam Silverberg told me to look up his radical group in New York. You'll have friends, he said, and lots of things to do. "Like organizing my uncle's workers?" I said. He laughed; "No, gar-

ment workers already have a union. But lots of others don't."
I promised to write Miss Shaughnessy regularly. And Nina?
After a hard good-bye, I would never see her again . . .

I stayed with my grandparents in the Bronx. I felt like a
stranger there; I had seen so little of them over the years. And
now they looked ancient to me, unreachable. We exchanged
hardly a word after the first welcome. I rode the crowded steamy
subway into Manhattan early every morning, reporting to the
job by eight. I had no skills and no appetite for his business, so
my uncle didn't bother to train me for anything. He set me to
stretching lengths of fabric on a long, long table, on which the
skilled cutters then laid out patterns and carved out with their
electric machines the pieces the dresses would be made up of.
The air was hot and close, the windows grimy, the floor littered
with scraps, everyone rushing about frantically as though some
invisible slave-driver were cracking his whip at their backs. I
found it hard to get to know anyone working in the shop. Their
life, their work, their interests were so different from mine, I
assumed, perhaps wrongly,—and besides, I was too shy to make
the first advance. My uncle was just as demanding of me as of
anyone else. I had only a half hour for lunch; I wolfed down
the sandwich Grandma had prepared, then ran out to the streets
to soak myself in the city life. The size and noise of the crowds
packed into every block at lunchtime stunned me.

I pushed my way through, trying to see what lay on the edge
of the garment district. Heading north a few blocks, I found
myself in the theater district. Dozens of playhouses, their bright
posters announcing comedies, dramas, the musicals of George
Gershwin and Cole Porter and Jerome Kern, the D'Oyly Carte
company in Gilbert & Sullivan, the Abbey Players from Dublin
doing O'Casey and Synge. And Shakespeare and Congreve and
Wilde and O'Neill and Rice and Behrman and Hellman . . . A

feast I longed to gorge myself on. But how? With what? The cheapest seats in the balcony were 55 cents, but I couldn't afford to spend that much. I figured out an angle. I worked till 1 P.M. on Saturdays. Then I'd brush the lint off my clothes, wash my face, comb my hair, and walk over to a theater. Hang around till the first act ended, and the audience came out on the sidewalk for the intermission. Move casually among them and as the bell rang to announce the second act, stroll inside with the others, stand in the back till the house lights began to dim, then take an empty seat as though it belonged to me . . .

It worked. And for years. Of course, I missed all the first acts. But I knew the plot-lines from reading the published plays, and the modern ones I knew from the *Times* reviews. It was my free course in world drama.

There was little time to read. My hours were long, the work tedious and tiring, and the subway back up to the Bronx in the sweltering summer evenings drained what energy was left. "Stay home and rest!" Grandma would say on Sunday, but I couldn't wait to explore the city. I wanted to learn every neighborhood, see every sight, taste every pleasure. My favorite ride was to catch the double-decker Fifth Avenue bus at the north end of Riverside Drive, and sit on the open top deck, watching the ferries crossing the Hudson and the sailboats skimming the water, and admiring the mansions and big apartment houses on the Drive. On my first trip, I saw strung along the Hudson shore hundreds of shacks made of tin cans, packing crates, cardboard, and old tar paper. They were no bigger than chicken coops, these rent-free homes, and their tenants had named them Hoovervilles in honor of the President.

As that hot and lonely summer wore on, the papers were showing Hoovervilles of another kind sprawled on the outskirts of Washington. Nearly 20,000 veterans, dubbed the Bonus Army, had flooded into the capital to demand payment of a veterans' bonus. It wasn't due till 1945, but over a quarter of a million ex-soldiers—jobless and hungry—needed that money now. Hoover opposed paying them. They squatted in all kinds of cockeyed lean-tos scraped together from the city dump. Congress quit for the summer without paying them their bonus, but the vets hung on. Then Hoover ordered infantry, cavalry, tanks, and machine guns to get rid of them. This was long before television. The papers showed pictures, but you could see what it was truly like only in the newsreels in the movie theaters. I saw the unarmed vets with their shelters burned, their food destroyed, and two of them shot dead. They fled Washington, stumbling along the roads back to where they had come from.

What Hoover wanted was to make the country believe the danger of revolution was real, and that America needed him because he was prepared to crush a revolution. The Republicans had already renominated him for President. The Democrats chose Franklin D. Roosevelt. Too absorbed with New York, I didn't pay much attention to the election campaign, except to hear one or two speeches on the radio. Hoover's tone struck me as mournful, hopeless, while FDR radiated confidence in his ability to make things better. This man isn't going to let people starve, I thought.

I spent one Saturday afternoons wandering around the campus at Columbia. It seemed enormous to me, running from 114th Street up to 120th Street, all red brick and white stone, with separate buildings devoted to such departments as law and philosophy and architecture and physics and chemistry and engineering and journalism. I found the dormitory I already knew I'd live in, come September. It was John Jay Hall, a tall building at the southeast corner of the campus. Tennis courts fronted it, I was happy to see, and a big playing field with a track. Far up at the opposite end was Teachers College, whose facilities New College would share. Its halls and classrooms were jammed with summer students from everywhere, working for graduate credits. Young women especially, and in vast number and variety.

I did not know what would happen next. All around me were the signs of collapse. More people than ever suspended in a void, without work, without income, without hope. Anxiety and fear were thick in the American air. Suicide, murder, desertion, despair, the symptoms of a society's breakdown. There were more bread riots and hunger marches that summer. Some politicians and papers feared revolution was around the corner. Radicals like Adam hoped or believed it was. Like most Americans, I was not ready for that. I wanted change, but did not know what kind, or who or what would bring it about. The most I could hope for was that FDR would make a difference.

The summer ended and with it my job. Only then did I realize that I had been working in the same trade as my mother long ago, and my grandfather, too. It was a link of some kind, however brief, to family history and it made me feel good. Now it was over. I stuffed my clothing and books into a bag, kissed Grandma and Grandpa good-bye, and checked into John Jay Hall at Columbia. It was September 1932, and I was seventeen.

Afterword

This is my early life as I see it now. I can't pretend to know exactly how it was when I was five or fifteen. Inevitably the story is colored by what I have become this many years later. The writer's imagination is always remaking the real, even as he struggles to be as honest as he can.

How much is left out? I can't be sure, for everybody's memory of childhood is shaky. There is more than family here; we all grow up in a community. Worcester, too, counts in the story. Many of the things and people I came across in my hometown found their way into the books I would write long after. Back then, I didn't know I would be a writer. Yet something was going on there to shape my interests and my point of view.

Some of the names in this book have been changed, and some of the circumstances. So the book is part fact and part fiction. I kept no diary nor do any letters survive. But even if there were such documents, how convincing would this evidence be as proof of the reality? They, too, would be words, and words are always selected and manipulated to achieve an effect.

Sometimes in this book I've given up fact and taken to fiction—not to avoid the truth, but to capture it.

In many of the books written by Milton Meltzer, you can hear the echoes of his experiences growing up in Worcester, Massachusetts. He has written about the Great Depression of the Thirties as well as about poverty today, about slavery in America and the lives of the abolitionists who struggled to overthrow it. His series on ethnic groups includes the Native Americans, and the Jewish, Chinese, Hispanic and black Americans. For the *Women of Our Times* series, he has told the stories of social activists Mary McLeod Bethune, Winnie Mandela, Betty Friedan, and Dorothea Lange. His biographies for older readers include Langston Hughes, Henry David Thoreau, Mark Twain, George Washington, and Benjamin Franklin.

After attending Columbia University, Meltzer worked as a writer for the WPA Federal Theater Project and then served in the Air Force in World War II. He has written for newspapers, magazines, films, and television. The first of his more than 70 books, *A Pictorial History of Black Americans* (1956), written with Langston Hughes, is still in print. His many honors include five nominations for the National Book Award. He has also won the Christopher, Jane Addams, Carter G. Woodson, Jefferson Cup, Washington Book Guild, Olive Branch, and Golden Kite awards.

He and his wife Hildy, parents of two daughters, Jane and Amy, live in New York City. A grandson, Benjamin Meltzer McArthur, has recently joined the family.